A soft smile on her ... the sunset as it slow... the horizon.

Cayden forced his eyes to glance out over the water, hoping the sound of the small waves breaking against the shoreline soothed the restlessness in him as it usually did. But he couldn't focus on anything other than the woman sitting next to him. She rested her chin atop her knees and stared out at the water with deep appreciation. He knew how she felt. He felt the same way looking at her.

"So breathtakingly beautiful," she said.

"Anytime you want to watch the sunset from the beach, just call."

Her gaze cut to him, and after a moment, she smiled. "I... Thank you, Cayden. For, well, for an enjoyable evening. It's been really nice."

"It has been a nice evening." He stared into her eyes and fought the desire to lean in to kiss her. *Much too soon for that,* he told himself. But that didn't change the fact that he wanted to kiss her. Badly.

Dear Reader,

Have you ever wished you could just do a complete makeover on your life? That perhaps the choices you've made haven't been the best ones and you just want to wipe the slate clean and start over? There have definitely been times during my life that I'd have answered yes to those questions.

Having gone from foster care to adoption to losing her new parents at a young age, Dr. Hailey Easton clung to a bad relationship for much too long to give herself a sense of not being alone in the world. Fortunately, she breaks free and moves to Florida, where she plans to experience life.

Cardiologist Cayden Wilton is a heart expert but has never found the right person to share his with. Now he's falling for a woman who claims not to want his heart. Will he be able to convince her that his love can mend the broken pieces of her life?

I hope you enjoy Cayden and Hailey's love story. I sure enjoyed writing it. Take care.

Love,

Janice Lynn

FLIRTING WITH THE FLORIDA HEART DOCTOR

JANICE LYNN

Harlequin

MEDICAL ROMANCE

Harlequin®
MEDICAL
ROMANCE

ISBN-13: 978-1-335-94276-0

Recycling programs for this product may not exist in your area.

Flirting with the Florida Heart Doctor

Harlequin Enterprises ULC
22 Adelaide St. West, 41st Floor
Toronto, Ontario M5H 4E3, Canada
www.Harlequin.com

Printed in U.S.A.

USA TODAY and Wall Street Journal bestselling author **Janice Lynn** has a master's in nursing from Vanderbilt University and works as a nurse practitioner in a family practice. She lives in the southern United States with her Prince Charming, their children, their Maltese named Halo and a lot of unnamed dust bunnies that have moved in after she started her writing career. Readers can visit Janice via her website at www.janicelynn.com.

Books by Janice Lynn

Harlequin Medical Romance

A Surgeon to Heal Her Heart
Heart Surgeon to Single Dad
Friend, Fling, Forever?
A Nurse to Tame the ER Doc
The Nurse's One Night to Forever
Weekend Fling with the Surgeon
Reunited with the Heart Surgeon
The Single Mom He Can't Resist
Heart Doctor's Summer Reunion
Breaking the Nurse's No-Dating Rule
Risking It All with the Paramedic

Visit the Author Profile page
at Harlequin.com for more titles.

**Janice won the National Readers' Choice Award
for her first book,
The Doctor's Pregnancy Bombshell.**

To Kimberly Bradford Scott. You're amazing.

CHAPTER ONE

DR. HAILEY EASTON didn't like the cold. Tired of northern Ohio winters, her past life, and the toxic relationship she'd left behind, she welcomed Venice, Florida's sunshine. However, when she'd moved south, she'd been thinking of warm weather and new beginnings, not her heated reaction to Dr. Cayden Wilton.

Having never experienced such awareness, Hailey's instant attraction to the cardiologist coming down the hallway wasn't something she could have foreseen, especially not after the drawn-out ten-year destruction of her belief in the opposite sex. Sometimes life threw in surprises. Her surprises had rarely been good ones, but things were going to be different in Florida.

Things were already different.

With a complete head-to-toe makeover, *she* was different. It was more than just her outer appearance that had changed. She was lighter, freer, and determined to shake her past. In her new sunshine-filled life she planned to erase the wasted years of John demolishing her already miniscule self-confidence and making her believe she hadn't deserved anything better than what little he'd given. Since she'd stayed for so long in the relationship, hoping he'd change, maybe she hadn't. Either way, with finishing medical school and acknowledging that it was now or never, she'd said goodbye to her old self, Ohio, John, and to silly dreams. Hello, Florida and the improved Hailey.

"I see who you're looking at and you're wasting your time." Her coworker Renee confirmed what Hailey had known. Dr. Wilton was way out of her league.

No, stop that, she scolded herself.

She wouldn't let John's voice reign any longer.

Being realistic wasn't being negative, though. Hailey was no beauty queen, but she had a good heart, loved people, and as far as looks, well, she had nice teeth and had always liked her eyes. They were her best feature, in her opinion, which was fitting as one's eyes were the window to one's soul. Thanks to the corrective eye surgery she'd gifted herself as a finishing-residency present, her thick glasses no longer obscured that window. Even with her radical revamping, she was more along the lines of an average, slightly overweight person, and not someone who turned heads. Cayden Wilton must be a leading cause of whiplash. The man was gorgeous.

"He's taken," Renee continued, glancing from the cardiologist to Hailey.

Just as well; she'd made her move to work on herself, to find her inner happiness, not to jump into another relationship. When she was ready to date again, it would be light, fun, about her, and she could play in any league that valued the things that mattered most.

"Taken?" Asking was way outside the old Hailey's comfort zone, but she couldn't hold back her curiosity, so maybe all those self-help books she'd been devouring were working. Dr. Wilton hadn't been wearing a wedding ring, but that didn't mean he was single. Of course, he wasn't. Like John, Dr. Wilton was one of the beautiful people of the world—everyone flocked to them with no effort on their part.

"Claimed would be a more accurate description," the charge nurse clarified from where she sat next to Hailey in the small open office cubby behind the nurses' station. The hospital walls were a light gray and were offset with stark white ceilings and trim. White tiled floors added to the calming, clean feel. The unit boasted a fresh clean linen scent that was a positive testament to housekeeping. "When he is ready to settle down, everyone expects him to marry Leanna

Moore, especially Leanna. They're the hospital's very own 'celebrity' couple. We refer to them as Caydna."

Caydna? Venice General Hospital's drama was on a whole new level. She couldn't recall any couple name combos at her Ohio hospital other than someone occasionally referring to "Bennifer," "Brangelina," or "Tayvis" celebrity couples.

Hailey had seen Dr. Wilton three times. Once from across the hospital cafeteria during her orientation, yesterday during her first shift as Venice General's newest inpatient physician, and right now. Each time, she'd wondered if she was hitting menopause prior to her thirtieth birthday as she instantly flushed hot.

Dragging her gaze from the scrub-wearing cardiologist walking down the med-surg unit's hallway was impossible. Tall, athletically built, gorgeous hazel eyes, and brown, slightly wavy hair, he commandeered her attention and refused to let go.

As Cayden passed, Sharla Little rushed from her husband's room, calling out to him. Melvin Little had required an emergency appendectomy for a ruptured appendix the previous night. After Hailey rounded on him at his transfer to the medical/surgical floor that morning, she had entered the cardiac consult to keep close tabs on his significant history of congestive heart failure. Now, fatigue and worry etched upon her face, Mrs. Little swiped at the tears that had started. Whatever she said had Cayden placing his arm around her shoulder and giving a hug. His unabashed show of compassion surprised Hailey. Good-looking, smart, and kind.

"Leanna Moore?" Why had Hailey spoken on his personal life? She did not want to get caught up in hospital gossip. As she said the name out loud an image of a pretty blonde on a billboard popped into her mind. "The radio personality?"

"The one and only."

Embarrassed she'd voiced an interest, Hailey forced her gaze to the computer screen where she should be addressing messages—she had a ton of new employee ones filling her inbox.

"It doesn't surprise me that you know who Leanna is despite having just moved to the area a few weeks ago. Born and raised here, she's Venice's darling. She wants Dr. Wilton and doesn't care who knows it. After they met at a charity event, she convinced him to do a weekly heart health segment during her morning show. He doesn't go out with any woman more than a few times, but Leanna lasted several months and they've kept in touch since, which makes her different from all the rest. Of course, their continued relationship may just be that he's a softie for raising money for the needy or promoting a good cause. I think he sits on every volunteer committee the hospital has."

"That's admirable."

Watching where Dr. Wilton still spoke with Mrs. Little, Renee nodded. "He's admirable. In lots of ways that go beyond that fabulous smile of his. Despite his playboy reputation, we all adore him and most of us have crushed on him."

Hailey arched a brow at the nurse who'd claimed to be happily married when they'd been chitchatting the previous day. "Even you?"

"Touché." Renee leaned back in her chair and grinned. "Not crush, per se, but my eyes can see. Mmm-hmm. He is fine."

Hailey smiled as the fifty-something woman fanned her face.

"So, what you're saying is that for a fun, no-strings-attached evening I should invite him to check out that tiki bar in Manasota that you were telling me about?" She had no intentions of doing so, had never asked out a man, but teasing Renee was fun. Even thinking that someday she might be so bold was mind-boggling. She'd always been demure, letting John dictate their relationship, and doing her best to keep the peace. That hadn't worked out well.

Renee's eyes widened as did her smile. "I tell you what, new girl, you forget everything I said and you have your fun. Just keep your heart in check so it doesn't get broken."

Her heart had already been broken. Just once, because she'd only had one romantic relationship. It had been a long and painful breaking, piece by shattered piece.

Taking a deep breath and forcing a smile, Hailey shook her head. "I was joking, but like you, my eyes appreciate beauty. Dr. Wilton looks as if he belongs on a television medical drama rather than in a real hospital. He'd be an instant heartthrob." Ha ha. Look at her making a pun with his being a cardiologist. As far as her own heart, when and if she dated again, she'd keep it locked up tighter than Fort Knox. "Now, tell me about these volunteer committees and charities. I want to get involved in my new hometown."

She wanted to do more, to give back more, to focus on things beyond just remaking herself, but to also contribute to making the world a better place. In Ohio, John hadn't wanted her to have a life outside of residency and their relationship. Looking back, she was ashamed of how she'd let him rob her of so much joy. She had gifts to give and wanted to do just that. That volunteering was a great way to meet people and make friends was an added bonus.

Eyes twinkling, Renee turned toward where Cayden was stepping behind the nurses' station counter. "Good morning, Doctor Wilton. Saw you talking with Mrs. Little. Do I need to enter new orders?" She jerked her thumb toward Hailey. "Also, Dr. Easton wants to volunteer with Venice Has Heart. Can you help her?"

Hailey's jaw dropped. *That* was not what she'd meant when she'd asked about the charities. She never should have teased Renee.

Cayden's gaze shifted toward them, going first to Renee, then settling on Hailey. An amused light shone in his gorgeous eyes. His lips curved, digging dimples into his cheeks that matched the one on his chin. The man had a strong, yet friendly facial structure. From what Hailey could tell, he had great everything, but she'd been wrong before.

"You want to volunteer for Venice Has Heart?" he asked.

She didn't even know what Venice Has Heart was, but that didn't stop her from saying, "Renee thinks I should and suggested I talk to you about doing so." Hailey glanced toward the charge nurse who looked all innocent although she was far from it, then returned her attention to him. "Where do I find out more?"

"That's great. We're always looking for more volunteers." His phone dinged and he glanced down at the message that appeared on his watch face. "Sorry, one sec." Brows veeing, he typed out a quick response, then smiled at Hailey, causing a major rhythm hiccup. "As far as where to find out more, I'd love to tell you about Venice Has Heart. I've got to round on a few patients, then get back to the clinic, but maybe we can meet this evening, I can give you the lowdown then."

Hailey's face heated. Meet that evening? How long was giving her the "lowdown" going to take? Unless he was using her volunteering as an excuse to make plans with her and if so, how did she feel about that? She'd just moved to Florida a few weeks before. She'd intended to focus on building a life, not a romantic relationship.

Drastic makeover or not, she knew Cayden was just being kind as he had been with Sharla Little. She shouldn't read anything into his invitation other than at face value he wanted to tell a new colleague about a beloved charity.

Beside her, Renee elbowed her arm. "Hailey was just saying she wanted to try out that fabulous tiki bar in Manasota and check out some of our Florida nightlife." Her coworker smiled big at Dr. Wilton. "Maybe you could have dinner, listen to the band, watch the sunset, tell her about Venice Has Heart, and all the reasons why moving to our little sunny part of the world was a great decision."

The hospital floor could just open and swallow Hailey, chair and all. The sooner, the better. But Cayden didn't seem to mind. If anything, he seemed intrigued by Renee's comment.

"That sounds like a great idea." He looked directly at Hailey, making her forget to breathe as she stared into eyes that were a deep green with golden flecks and rimmed with an intense blue. "Shall I pick you up at six?"

Feeling panicky, she reminded herself that it was just an innocent meeting between colleagues to discuss a volunteer opportunity and shook her head. "My shift ends at six, Dr. Wilton, but I'll meet you there at seven." Look at her taking charge with the time suggestion. Such a small thing, but after years of following John's dictates, pride filled her that she hadn't just said yes.

"It's Cayden. Thought I mentioned that yesterday," he said, his smile revving up her heart rate even more. His phone dinged a second time, and, glancing down at his watch to view the message, he sighed. "Sorry. Duty calls. I'm going to see Mr. Little and the other cardiac consult." He shot one last smile toward her. "Looking forward to seeing you at seven, *Hailey*."

"Okay." She didn't say *Cayden* back, couldn't even wrap her brain around doing so, which was silly. She'd been on a first-name basis with coworkers in the past. But saying Cayden's name out loud felt as if it would be more than something casual and not something she should do in front of Renee.

What is wrong with me?

He moved to leave the nurses' station area to head down the hospital hallway. Renee grabbed her arm, giving an excited squeeze, and mouthed, "Girl!" However, the nurse rapidly straightened when Cayden turned back toward them, standing just to the other side of the counter separating the nurses' area from the hallway but still in close proximity of the office cubby along the back wall. A fresh heatwave infused Hailey's face because no way had he missed Renee's theatrical shimmy.

His gaze dropped to where Renee's fingers wrapped around her arm, then lifted to Hailey. A twinkly light shone there, making the golden flecks glisten. "We should exchange numbers in case something comes up and one of us is running late."

"Or if one of us needs to cancel."

His brow lifted. "Changing your mind already?"

"I meant in case you were too busy to meet and just wanted to call."

"Why would I do that?" He made it sound as if the idea was preposterous.

Taking a deep breath, she cleared her throat.

"You're a cardiologist. I can think of a few scenarios that could prevent you from meeting me."

"A few," he agreed, grinning as he handed her his phone to punch in her number. "But I'm not on call tonight, so we should be good. I was more concerned that you might get hung up here at shift change." A realistic possibility, she thought as she typed in her number with shaky fingers. He took the phone, glanced down at what she'd input, then hit Dial, causing her phone to vibrate in her scrub pocket. "Now you have my number, too. I'm looking forward to a relaxing evening of a good food, music, sunset, and great company. See you at seven."

This time when he turned to leave, it was a stunned, wobbly-legged Hailey grabbing Renee's arm.

"I thought you weren't on call tonight," Hailey reminded Cayden from where she sat catty-corner from him at an outdoor table at The Manasota Mango. After he'd pulled out her chair and waited for her to sit, she'd thought he'd move across from her. Instead, he'd chosen the closer seat to where they could both easily see the band on the far end of the outdoor patio. When the hostess had seated them, he'd requested to be in easy line of vision, but not so close that the music would be too loud for them to hear each other when talking. The young lady had chosen the perfect spot.

"I'm not." Cayden slid the phone back into his pocket. "But, as you could tell, that was the hospital. You know how it is. In our profession, you're always working on some level. I like to keep up-to-date on any changes in my hospitalized patients."

Taking a sip of the fruity nonalcoholic drink she'd ordered, Hailey nodded. She did know how it was for many in her profession. With solely overseeing inpatient care as a hospitalist, she didn't get a ton of after-hour calls. At least, she hadn't in Ohio as a resident and wasn't expecting to in Florida.

Although she'd been nervous when she'd first arrived at the restaurant, she'd mostly relaxed as they'd eaten their meal and chatted, assuring herself that Cayden's invitation had been nothing more than a casual one of convenience for telling her about Venice Has Heart. His easy laughs, frequent compliments, and seeming fascination with whatever she said was enough to make a woman's head spin, though.

"That was Dr. Bentley who came on at the end of your shift," he continued. "Melvin Little has increased shortness of breath. Dr. Bentley ordered a chest X-ray and additional labs. He questioned if there were any other tests that I'd like done prior to my rechecking Melvin in the morning."

"Sorry to hear that his breathing has worsened." Neither Melvin nor his wife had mentioned anything when she'd rounded prior to the end of her shift. "I'll be there in the morning."

"Ah, so if you completely avoid me, I'll know I failed miserably tonight." His eyes twinkled.

She made a noise that was a somewhat embarrassing cross between a snort and laugh. "You already know you're a success. Your passion for educating our community on heart health through a fun event completely wowed me. All you're missing is my name signed on the dotted line to have me locked in for a full day of providing medical consults with anyone who has an abnormal screen."

"I'll bring the ironclad contract in the morning," he teased. "My grandfather died of a heart attack when I was young. I've often wondered how different things would have been if he'd just known how to take care of himself, things like a proper diet and lifestyle habits." His expression had gone momentarily serious, then he smiled. "But you're right. Tonight is a success because I got to spend time getting to know you."

Remember what Renee said. Have fun, but don't take him too seriously.

"Yes, since we'll be seeing each other with

the Venice Has Heart event." Cheeks burning, she took another sip of her pineapple and coconut drink, thinking maybe she should have gone for the real deal for liquid courage. She'd not wanted to dull her senses while talking to him in hopes that she would be less likely to say or do silly things. But, being with him, knowing people were looking their way and likely wondering why he was with her, twisted her stomach into knots.

Quit, she reminded herself. *Quit. Quit. Quit. Cayden asked you here, is smiling at you, and seems to be enjoying himself. Being with him was great practice for if you ever do risk dating again.*

Just like her "as friends" Saturday night plans with a neighbor was great practice. She'd bumped into Ryan several times at neighborhood events and the gym. His offer to introduce her to his friend group had been kind and she looked forward to the cookout. When ready, she'd need all the help she could get she'd not been on a first date in ten years. Although she and John had officially called their relationship quits with Hailey moving into their guest bedroom three months prior to leaving Ohio, she'd not dated. Having done so in Ohio would have antagonized an already bad situation. Not to mention that she'd had zero interest. Apparently, the Florida sunshine was thawing something inside her, though, because her body was logging all kinds of interest where Cayden was concerned.

"You'll definitely be seeing me with Venice Has Heart." His smile deepened his dimples.

"Um, yeah." Hailey gulped. She was a novice when it came to men, but good grief, what she saw in his eyes. His gaze burned so hot it was a wonder she didn't spontaneously combust. "I look forward to volunteering. I love that you have the local nursing programs involved to take blood pressures and random blood sugar readings."

Could she sound any cornier? She wasn't used to having dinner with gorgeous single, flirty men. The emotions hitting her and having to deal with them weren't things she could learn about from her self-help books, that was for sure.

"It's a great experience for them on a lot of different levels as they get real-world experience. Their instructors always provide positive feedback that the students have shared."

"Anytime one can get hands-on experience is a good thing. The band is good."

His brow arched. "Do you like classic rock?"

Although somewhat familiar with it, she didn't even know the name of the song that was currently being sung. "I like most music," she answered honestly. "But even if not my favorite genre, I appreciate the band's musical skills.

They're talented, don't you think?" She smiled. Wasn't that what her books said to do and to do frequently? Smile because a smile went a long way to making most situations better.

"They are." Something in the way that he said it made her wonder if he had paid any more attention to what song was playing than she had. "What's your favorite genre?"

For years Hailey had listened to rap because that had been John's favorite. Her favorite hadn't been something she'd thought much about, maybe ever. For far too long she hadn't thought about what her favorite anything was. No more. In her new life, she was finding herself, her likes, and her dislikes. She'd never be purposefully oppositional, but she wasn't going to be a doormat ever again. She considered what she'd listened to while she'd been unpacking her few belongings into the house she'd bought not too far from where they currently were. "I listen to a variety of music, but when alone, I tend to listen to pop. I'm going with that as my favorite."

"When you're not concerned about whether or not someone else is enjoying what is playing, you listen to pop." His observation was so on the money that she blushed. He took a drink from his bottle, then placed it back on the table. "Who is your favorite artist?"

"Elvis," she said without hesitation, smiling as

memories assailed her of listening to the Memphis crooner with the couple who'd rescued her from bouncing from one foster family to another. He'd been her adopted parents' favorite and she'd grown up listening to him and other iconic performers from the sixties and seventies. She'd been eleven when she'd been adopted by the older couple who'd never had children of their own. Hailey equated the singer with having a home and a family because she never had prior to being introduced to his silky voice.

Cayden chuckled. "Not what I was expecting you to say. As the known King of Rock 'n' Roll and not a pop artist, I have to ask, why Elvis?"

"Why not Elvis? After all, like you said, he is the 'King of Rock 'n' Roll.' But if you meant a more modern artist or band, I'll go with Ed Sheeran."

"Nice. I saw him in concert back during my early college days," he surprised her by saying, although she wasn't sure why she was surprised. No doubt Cayden had an active social life that had included numerous concerts over the years. "He is a super-talented musician. My friends and I had a great time."

"He did a show in Columbus at the beginning of my freshman year. A group of classmates sold a kidney or two to come up with enough money to go see him and invited me to tag along." She smiled at the memory, trying not to question herself too much on why she'd let John systematically cut her off from everyone in her life. With moving from one foster home to another and her adopted parents opting to homeschool her, she'd never had any close friendships. She had been thrilled when her classmates had asked her to go with them to the concert. She'd thought she was on top of the world—making friends and having a boyfriend for the first time ever. The concert had been one of her few friend outings. John had thrown a fit. He'd thrown a fit for her breaking things off and moving to Florida, too, telling her she'd regret leaving and come running home, lonely and begging for his forgiveness for her "stupidity." There was no level of loneliness that would send her back to him. Being with John the past ten years had been some of her loneliest and with her childhood, that was saying something. Thank God she'd had her lifelong dream of being a doctor to focus on and keep her from sinking into despair.

"Willing to sacrifice body parts for great music—making a note of it," Cayden teased, taking a sip of his drink and pulling her back to the present. A present where she had achieved her greatest goal and now planned to heal the holes in who she was, to get to know that person, and learn to love herself completely and know that she was enough and didn't need anyone else in her life. "You went to school in Columbus?"

"I had a scholarship to Ohio State for my undergraduate studies. Staying for medical school made sense." John had been there. After her parents died, without him she would have been completely alone in the world, as he'd pointed out on a regular basis. Looking back, she wondered what her life would have been like if she'd left Ohio. Better in many ways, but she had learned powerful lessons. She hadn't been a fast learner, but she had eventually caught on. She'd never wear that in-a-serious-relationship cage again. "What about you? Are you originally from Florida?"

Cayden took another drink from his bottle. "I grew up around Gainesville, did residency in Kentucky and a fellowship in Kansas. I missed the ocean enough to know I didn't want to live anywhere that didn't offer a sunset over the water."

Having already fallen in love with being near the sea, Hailey understood. She ran her finger over condensation forming on her glass. The moisture was cool beneath her fingertips and as welcome as the breeze cutting the evening's heat. "Because sunsets are what you like best about being near the ocean?"

"More that I wanted to remind you that Renee

mentioned our watching the sunset." He grinned in a way that had Hailey gulping. His smile was lethal. Maybe he couldn't help himself and just naturally flirted with every woman. Not that she'd seen him do so with anyone else, not even the hostess who'd definitely given him the eye. "I'm fine with staying here, listening to the band," he continued. "Or we could walk across the street and watch the sunset from the beach. There are just enough clouds in the sky that the colors should be spectacular."

A spectacular sunset over the water with a gorgeous man sounded surreal. Scary, too. But Hailey had moved to Florida to be different, to step outside her comfort zone, and to create the life she wanted. That life should include spectacular sunsets.

"Watching the sun set while sitting on the beach would be great and something I've not done since moving here."

He feigned horror. "What? How is that even possible? That should have been one of the first things anyone who moves here does."

"It's not that I haven't wanted to." She glanced toward the band who'd started singing a Lynyrd Skynyrd classic. "But I wasn't sure how safe it would be for me to be on the beach and walk back to my car by myself after dark. I've not heard of any safety issues, but I'm new to the area and trying to make good choices, not put myself in compromising situations."

Unlike the past. She'd made a terrible choice with John and compromised for almost a decade. Had she stayed so long because she'd been grieving her parents, in school, then in residency, and she just hadn't had the energy to break free? Was that why she'd turned a blind eye and forgiven so many things? Or had the fear of being alone kept her there?

"I doubt you'd have any problems, but it's always best to be safe." Cayden finished his drink, placed the bottle on the table, then motioned for their waitress to bring their check. Hailey reached for her purse, pulled out her wallet, but Cayden shook his head. "Tonight is my treat."

Clutching her wallet, she met his gaze and hoped her face wasn't as rosy as it felt. "I don't expect you to pay for my meal."

His brows scrunched together. "When a man invites you to dinner, you should expect him to pay. My advice is that if he expects you to pay, next time, tell him to hit the road."

"Duly noted." She was so used to paying for everything with John that she'd just automatically planned to do the same. John's thoughts had been that she should just be grateful for the opportunity to support him. If she'd let him, he would have broken her financially the way he had her heart. Fortunately, most of her parents' estate had been tied up until a few months back. Acid burned her throat, and she took another sip of the virgin drink, letting the cold liquid glide down her throat to ease the heat. The fruity sweetness did little to dissolve her bitterness at her own foolishness that she'd once again let John into her head. Maybe it was natural for him to pop into her mind since tonight was the first time she'd ever had dinner with a man who wasn't John.

"To be fair, though, Renee instigated our dinner tonight."

Cayden shook his head. "Renee might have made the initial suggestion, but I asked. Dinner is my treat."

"In that case, thank you." She slipped her slim wallet back into her cross-body and assured herself that it was okay that she was letting him pay even though doing so felt awkward. The new her did not pay when she met a man for dinner. Okay, got it. "For the record, what about if I ask someone to dinner? Who should I expect to pay then?"

Not that she'd probably ever be so bold, but this new Florida Hailey was a work in progress. She refused to be boring, walked-all-over Ohio Hailey ever again. Talking with Cayden was insightful and wonderful and reinforced that she'd been right to start fresh in a place of her choosing. The hospitalist position in Venice had been a godsend.

Cayden shrugged. "That one is okay either way. If he insists, its fine for you to let him pay. But he doesn't lose points if he lets you since you asked." He paused, then added, "Not the first time. If there's a second, call me old-fashioned, but he needs to man up."

It was difficult to think of the charming man sitting across from her as old-fashioned, but there was something about him that made her think he had an old soul. She liked whatever that something was.

"Tonight is enlightening." And an unexpected bonus to her new Florida life. "You're easy to talk to and seem quite the expert. Being new to the area, I should come to you for all my dating advice."

Hilarious. Unless one counted tonight, which she didn't since it wasn't one, she hadn't been on a first date in years. With the way John had shredded her heart, she might never risk letting someone in to mess with the woman she was working to become.

Certainly, she'd fight to protect the new her and would steer clear of anyone who threatened her hard-won peace. There were worse things than being alone.

She didn't need Cayden's, or anyone's, advice to know that.

Life had taught her that painful lesson well.

CHAPTER TWO

CAYDEN AND HAILEY crossed the street, paused at his SUV long enough to grab a blanket, then headed to the beach. When they reached the sand, he took off his shoes and Hailey did the same. Hot pink covered her toenails and her big toes each had a palm tree emblem in the middle of the polish. Liking the glimpse at her whimsy, Cayden grinned.

The Gulf's breeze whipped at her long blond hair, dancing the strands about her lovely face. She'd had her hair pulled back at the hospital. He loved that she'd loosened it for their dinner. She'd also changed and wore white capris, a bright blue top, and plain white canvas shoes.

Her heavily lashed eyes were cloudy with uncertainty, as if she was trying to decide if he'd really been eyeing her toenails. That he understood. He wasn't a feet guy, or at least, he never had been. But those brightly painted toenails were downright sexy. Of course, looking at her curvy figure, he couldn't name one part of Hailey that he didn't find attractive. She fascinated him, which explained why he was on the beach with a coworker. He liked women and wasn't shy about it, but he didn't spend personal time with women he worked with. Doing that was much too complicated when it didn't work out and it never worked out. He no longer wanted it to. He'd been cured of that ailment. He had a great life, was never lonely when he wanted company, and was completely happy with lifelong bachelorhood. He only spent time with women with an exit plan already in place, and never coworkers. Apparently, Hailey was the exception to that rule because none of that had kept him from asking her to dinner to discuss her volunteering with Venice Has Heart when he could have just sent her to their website.

"I'd thought it would be more crowded," Hailey mused as, their shoes dangling from their fingers and the blanket folded over his arm, they made their way across the warm sand.

"It's later in the day on a weeknight so not too busy, but it can get crowded at times." When they were about halfway to the water, he stopped. "This okay?"

She nodded, watching as he spread the blanket, then sat to face where the sun was making its descent toward the horizon. A seagull squawked in the distance and a couple of sandpipers darted to and fro at the edge of the surf. The golden light reflected off the water, casting a picturesque view for what was in many ways the most interesting evening he'd had in a long time. So long, in fact, that he couldn't recall having felt the excitement that buzzed through him when he looked at the woman next to him. He'd felt the buzz the first time he'd seen her and each time since. While grabbing something to eat with a colleague, he'd noticed the smiling blonde chatting with the hospital administrator. Yesterday, he'd practically tripped over introducing himself to her.

Hailey stared out at where small waves were racing ashore. She hugged her knees and appeared to relax to the calming sea sounds. He'd always found peace in being near the water and was pleased she seemed to do the same.

Hailey twisted toward him. The sun's setting rays cast a hue to her face, making the blue of her eyes seem almost electric. "Are you always this nice?"

"Nope." Take this moment for example. He felt more naughty than nice. "Why did the phrase, 'Nice guys finish last,' pop into my head?"

As he'd hoped, she smiled. "I can't imagine that you ever finish last."

"There have been times I've finished last." But not because he hadn't given his best effort.

"Look at you. You're a successful cardiologist and gor—" She paused. Her cheeks glowed brighter than the setting sun.

Suspecting what she was going to say and pleased that she thought so, he grinned. "Go on, Hailey. Finish what you were about to say."

Odd, as he wasn't one to fish for compliments, but he craved hers.

Her lips twitched. "I was going to say that you're easy on the eyes, but I stopped because I didn't want to give you a big head."

Her compliment did funny things to his chest, like make his heart jerk. What was it about her that made him feel as if he'd morphed back to high school days?

"You think I'm easy on the eyes?" he teased, but deep down, he admitted that he was encouraging her to elaborate because he still wanted to hear more.

"Don't pretend you're not aware. You've looked in a mirror. You know how blessed you are."

Interesting that her tone almost held accusation.

"I could say the same in regard to you," he said. She was a beautiful woman who took great care with her appearance, although he suspected that beneath the makeup she was just as stunning. Beneath the powder and paint, she had a natural beauty that shined through.

She rolled her eyes in a way that made him wonder if, when looking in her mirror, she saw the same person he did. He didn't think so. Which might explain why her cheeks turned such a rosy shade each time he complimented her, and she seemed so unaccustomed to the praise. Could she really not know how beautiful she was?

"Looks fade, Hailey. Mine, yours, everyone's. It's what's on the inside that matters."

"I agree with you, of course. But, in the real world, most people never look to see what's on the inside unless it's nicely packaged on the outside." Her words held too much hurt for them to be a casual observation point. Who had punched the holes in her? And why did the urge to patch those holes hit so hard? Not just repair the broken pieces, but to kintsugi them with the finest gold so that the new was better than the former version? They'd just met and he was not a white knight and didn't want to be.

"I'm not most people, Hailey." When her face remained serious, he added, "Just ask my mother and she'll gladly tell you all my finer points."

Her expression lightening, Hailey snorted. "Hmm, not sure I trust your mother to give an unbiased opinion. But I don't need to ask her because, surprisingly, I believe you."

"Thank you, I think." He chuckled, wondering if his own cheeks now matched the streaked sky. "I'm torn on whether that was a compliment or a backhanded insult."

"Compliment." She smiled a big, real smile that stole his breath, then turned to look at the water. The fading sunlight highlighted her features, showcasing her beauty that far outshone their surroundings.

"Then thank you," he told her.

She stared at where the sun was inching beneath the horizon's edge. Cayden couldn't drag his gaze from her. The breeze coming in off the Gulf ruffled her hair, and the sun's glow cast her in a golden hue that gave her an ethereal appearance, as if she couldn't possibly be real. Maybe she wasn't because she sure triggered otherworldly reactions.

"I can't believe I've not been coming out here in the evening when I'm so close. This is so peaceful, and feels safe." Cayden wouldn't call sitting next to her watching the sun go down "safe." *Dangerous* was the description that came to mind.

"You've ruined me," she continued. "I'm going to want to come back again and again."

"We can anytime you want. Being near the water is my thing and I don't mind company."

At least, he didn't tonight. Usually, he preferred being at the beach alone.

"Ha, after so many years of being landlocked, I may want to be out here day and night, but I promise I wasn't implying that we come together." She laughed. "There's something mesmerizing about the sound of the water, isn't there?"

There was something mesmerizing about the sound of her laughter, something that should have him leery of further developing a friendship with her. "Just let me know whenever you want company for a beach sunset or walk," he offered anyway. "Or we can go to Caspersen Beach to look for shark teeth. It's just down the coast and something a lot of folks around here enjoy."

Her eyes widened. "Look for shark teeth?"

He chuckled at her expression. "Did you not realize you moved to the shark tooth capital of the world?"

"The hospital forgot to list that in their job description. Does that mean there's more sharks here than anywhere else?" Her face squished. "For the record, that would not be a selling point for me. Although, I guess it's too late now since I'm here."

"Not sure about the number of sharks compared to other places, but the number of shark teeth has to do with the area having favorable conditions to fossilize the teeth. If you've never been shark tooth hunting, you're in for a treat."

"Ohio girl. I've never found a shark tooth, much less been shark tooth hunting. I didn't even know that was a thing or that there was a shark tooth capital of the world."

He tsked. "You can't live here and not ever go shark tooth hunting."

She eyed him. "You say that as if you're confident I'd find a shark tooth."

"I am."

Her expression grew suspicious. "Am I missing something? Are they just lying around on the sand or something?"

He laughed. "Sometimes you can find them lying on the beach. Here, too, for that matter, especially after a storm. But the best ones are in the water at Caspersen, even the occasional megalodon tooth can be found."

"You want me to hunt shark teeth *in the water* after you just told me the beach is the shark tooth capital of the world and that there are sharks?" She gave him an I-don't-think-so look. "No, thank you."

He couldn't resist teasing. "You'll be fine so long as you stay away from the teeth still attached to the shark."

She snorted and made a funny face that had him liking her more and more. "No worries there. I'm not knowingly going anywhere near a shark."

"Lucky for you then that the teeth we would be hunting aren't attached." He chuckled, thinking the lightness in her tone was more beautiful than any sunset he'd even seen.

"But they once were, so maybe shark tooth hunting isn't my thing. Although, I'll admit you have me intrigued that you're so confident I'd find one. I've never been that lucky on those types of things. I've never even found a four-leaf clover my whole life."

"Then your luck is about to change."

Her smile was slow, innocently seductive, as she said, "I'm tempted to say yes simply from curiosity, but then I recall what they say about curiosity and the cat."

"Fortunately, you're not a cat."

"Ha! When it comes to sharks, I admit to being a big scaredy-cat. I mean, I know they are just animals doing what nature intended, but nature also dictates my survival instinct to stay away."

"I promise to protect you."

Her humor faded, as did his, and his assurance felt like more than just part of their fun banter.

"I can protect myself." Her chin tilt dared him to say otherwise even as he recognized the forced gusto in her eyes. Wondering what, or who, had made her so prickly, Cayden longed for the return of lightness.

"Even from sharks?"

Taking a deep breath, she swallowed and relaxed a little. "I'll defer dealing with sharks to you."

"Good idea. You're acing this listening to advice thing." Too bad he wasn't listening to the warning bells going off in his own head about what he was doing with her, a coworker, watching the sunset on a beach, and flirting with her despite all the reasons he shouldn't.

"Being a good student was never a problem. It's the rest of life that I've struggled with." She sighed, then with a soft smile back on her face she rested her chin atop her knees and stared at the sunset with deep appreciation. "This is so much better than when I watched while sitting in my car."

Cayden wanted to know more, to know what struggles she'd faced, but sensed she wouldn't tell him, so kept his questions to himself. The thought of her sitting in her car, watching the sunset by herself, tugged at his insides.

Her gaze cut to him and after a moment, she smiled. "I...thank you, Cayden. For dinner, the expert dating advice—" her smile widened when she said that one "—for the sunset, for asking me to go shark tooth hunting, for making me feel happy, for, just, well, for an enjoyable evening with someone who I feel is a new friend. It's been really nice."

"Seriously, anytime you want to watch the sunset from the beach, just call. I'll meet you so you don't have to worry about being alone." For safety reasons. That was why he kept offering. To keep her safe.

Who was going to keep him safe from his growing attraction to her was another matter completely.

"Are you going to tell me about last night?"

Even prior to arriving at the hospital, Hailey had known Renee would ask about her evening with Cayden. What she hadn't known was what she wanted to share. How could she explain what she didn't understand. Despite his "playboy reputation," Cayden had been a perfect gentleman. She'd had a great time, even agreeing to go shark tooth hunting with him, because why not? The new her was supposed to be adventurous and open to new experiences. Shark tooth hunting, from the beach as she wouldn't be going in the water, would certainly be that. She wanted to make friends, to have a social life, and be involved with her community. Going with Cayden just made sense, right? So, why did butterflies dance her in her belly at the thought that she'd be spending more time with him?

Knowing she couldn't ignore Renee, she smiled. "We ate dinner, listened to the band, and discussed Venice Has Heart. Thank you for suggesting that. Venice Has Heart sounds like an amazing community outreach program."

"It is." Renee literally rubbed her hands together. "Now, tell me more. Being happily married as I am, I have to live vicariously through you when it comes to Cayden."

Attempting to look casual, Hailey shrugged. "There's nothing more to tell."

Renee jerked her head back in disbelief. "Oh, come on. You were with the hospital's most notorious bachelor and I saw how he looked at you yesterday like he wanted to devour you in one bite. There has to be something more to tell."

Hailey fought gulping at Renee's assessment. Cayden hadn't looked at her that way. Sure, there had been moments the night before when she'd swear his flirting went beyond friendliness and making a new coworker feel welcomed. But she couldn't convince herself that her makeover was so good that Cayden would be interested in her, and yet…no, his offer to meet her for future sunsets and to take her shark tooth hunting weren't date offers. As surprising as it was, Cayden had been easy to talk to, had made her smile, and was hopefully destined to be a friend. That he was the sexiest man she'd ever met had no bearing on how much she'd liked him other than to make her uncomfortably aware of her body's reaction to his hotness.

"I see you stalling. Tell me." Renee wasn't going to let up. Hailey's silent mulling had made it seem as if more had happened than what had, so she glanced up from where she'd been charting a note on the patient she'd seen first thing that morning.

Looking her coworker directly in the eyes, she smiled as big as her plumped-up lips would allow. "As you know, we met at the bar you recommended. The food and music were wonderful. He told me about Venice Has Heart. I'm volunteering for the event."

Renee frowned. "What about drinks and a sunset with our favorite cardiologist? Please tell me you didn't waste that fabulous opportunity by just talking shop all evening."

"You are who told me that he's already claimed for whenever he tires of being a bachelor." Did he have an emotional involvement with the radio deejay beyond friendship? Hailey hadn't gotten that impression. What she had gotten was the impression that he liked the shiny new her. Absently, she reached up to touch where she had her hair extensions pulled back. He'd sounded so sincere in his claim of outer beauty fading that she wondered what he'd think if he knew just how much she'd done to enhance her appearance. Would he have noticed Ohio Hailey? What was she thinking? She didn't want him to notice Florida Hailey. She wasn't in the market for a relationship. She wasn't ready for one. Only, she couldn't deny that his flirting had made her feel…good.

Renee's brows scrunched. "Yes, but Cayden is way in the future. No reason you can't have fun in the here and now."

"He seems like a great guy to be so involved with the event. I enjoyed dinner and talking with him, but I'm just coming out of a long and unhealthy relationship. I'm really not interested in anything more than friendship with any man." There. Maybe that truth would appease Renee because Hailey did like her and hoped their working relationship would develop into friendship. To say anything further was setting herself up for gossip. "I need to check on Melvin Little. Is Sharla with him this morning?"

Frustrated that Hailey wasn't telling her more, Renee sighed. "She barely leaves his side. She tells me they've been together for over fifty years."

"He's fortunate to have her." What would it be like to have someone who cared that much about you for that long? Sharla adored her husband and the sentiment seemed to be mutual. In many ways they reminded her of her adoptive parents. The Eastons had loved each other and given Hailey the only real affection she'd ever known. Prior to them, she'd been bounced from place to place from the point her birth mother had died from an overdose and if her birth mother had known who Hailey's father was, she'd not listed it on her birth certificate. When her adoptive mother had died from breast cancer, her father hadn't lived a year before succumbing to a heart attack. All the old feelings of being alone in the world had hit and she'd clung to John no matter what he did. As unhealthy as it had been, his was the longest relationship of her life. Maybe she could forgive herself a little for trying so hard to make things work.

"I was told that Dr. Wilton would be by this morning to check on him and the sick sinus syndrome patient in Room 204." Renee looked at Hailey as if she expected some type of reaction. If she got one, it would be over Hailey falling down memory lane, which felt more like nightmare street.

Meeting Renee's gaze was her only reaction to her coworker's comment.

"Great. With Mr. Little's ruptured appendix then surgery putting a toll on his body, his heart needs to be watched closely." She didn't mention that she already knew Cayden would be by. "Are you going with me to see him, then?"

"Do you need me to?" Renee crossed her arms, pouting a little that Hailey wasn't revealing what she wanted to hear and that, perhaps, Hailey truly had "wasted" the opportunity. What had Renee expected her to do? Make out with Cayden under the stars?

Knowing her color was rising and her co-worker was sure to notice, Hailey shook her head. "No, I was just checking."

Yikes. Her voice had broken a little.

"Then I'm going to stay here to do paperwork, maybe scribble notes on how you should have taken advantage of who you were with last night. Just because I told you to guard your heart didn't mean you couldn't have fun. Life is short. Sometimes you have to live a little." Renee waggled her brows. "Or a lot, if you get my drift."

Face aflame, Hailey grimaced. Yeah, that had never been that much fun for her. Maybe because it had always been about her trying to please John, doing whatever he wanted to try to make him so happy that he wouldn't want anyone else. Her best efforts hadn't worked, so maybe neither of them had been having much fun.

Knowing she had to get away from Renee's watchful eyes, Hailey headed to check on Melvin. Some of the medical floor rooms were doubles and some were private. Whether by luck or design, he was in a private room. Hailey knocked on the open door before stepping into the pale gray room with its white tiles. Although he was still on a liquid-only diet, the room smelled of oranges and Hailey noted peels on the wheeled bed tray that was pulled closer to Sharla than her husband. As long as his exam was okay, she planned to start him on bland soft foods that morning and would have Dietary bring breakfast.

"Good morning," she greeted as she took in the pale man lying in the hospital bed. He had the head of the bed raised and a couple of pillows stuffed behind him, propping himself up farther. He was in his midseventies, had thick white hair, and was too thin. All except his feet and ankles, which were swollen. They weren't weeping through the compression hose that she'd put on him the previous day, though. He hadn't been thrilled but hadn't had the energy to refuse. "How are you feeling today?"

"Like I'm starving and want to go home." He coughed. The cough had been wet, as if he'd needed to clear phlegm from his throat and struggled to do so.

"I'm hoping to do something about the starving part," she assured him, smiling. "As far as the going home, the charge nurse informed me that you had chest flutters last night and the night staff consulted with your cardiologist." Recalling where Cayden had been, who he'd been with during that consultation, Hailey's heart fluttered, too. "No symptoms since last night?"

Grunting as he cautiously scooted up farther on his hospital bed, Melvin shook his head. "I think it was just indigestion but after what happened with my stomach, I wasn't keeping quiet."

"Understood." His ruptured appendix had required his lower abdomen to be surgically opened and "cleaned" because he'd ignored his pain. Sepsis had quickly set in, increasing the criticalness of his situation. "How's your surgical site?"

He adjusted the white cotton hospital blanket covering him. "Okay, I guess. Just aggravating I had to have my appendix taken out. I thought that was something that happened to kids, not grown men."

She shrugged. "A bad appendix can happen at any age."

"Apparently," he muttered. "Too bad I didn't realize that was what was causing my pain. I thought I was trying to pass another kidney stone."

"Since both are painful, I understand how you could make that assumption. Besides my planning to let you eat, I've got more good news this morning. Your white blood cell count is trending downward so going home is getting closer."

Although he looked relieved, he grumbled, "No wonder with as much medication as you people have pumped into me."

"All those medications seem to be working." Hailey shifted her gaze to the tired-appearing woman sitting in the chair beside her husband's hospital bed. Had she eaten anything other than the orange? Hailey made a note to request Dietary bring an extra breakfast tray, if available. When Hailey had entered the room, Sharla's fingers had paused in the crocheting she was doing on making an afghan. The colors reminded Hailey of the previous night's sunset with its mix of warm red, orange, and golds. Her fingers itched to reach out to see if the yarn was as soft as it appeared. "That's beautiful."

Brightening at the compliment, Sharla held up the piece for Hailey to better see what she had done. "It's all my favorite colors. Working with my hands helps me not be so nervous at being here." Arranging the piece back into her lap, she chuckled. "I found that crocheting was good therapy years ago when we lived up north. I usually make several a year."

With med school, then residency, Hailey hadn't had time for hobbies since high school other than occasionally losing herself in a book. She hoped to find a few interests that would fill her with passion. Her adoptive mother had painted, and Hailey had dabbled with that on occasion during her teens. Wanting to please her talented mother who'd hoped Hailey would possess artistic ability, she'd never been able to relax enough to truly enjoy what she was doing, though. Hailey's talent had been reading, studying, and making excellent grades. She'd been great at doing those, but not so much on anything creative that she'd tried thus far in life. Maybe she'd try her hand at some new creative ventures, but for now, she was excited to learn more about her new hometown, to meet people, volunteer, and get involved in the community.

She wanted to have a life, because she'd not had one since…since before her parents died, since before John, and residency. Only during those few years after the Eastons adopted her up until they'd passed had she belonged anywhere and had a life.

With her move to Florida, she was changing that.

She examined Melvin, taking care with his surgical site as she checked the incision, and was glad that he continued to progress. "Let's see how you do with soft food, then we'll advance your diet as tolerated. If you don't have any reoccurrence of chest symptoms and your labs continue to improve when I review them in the morning, we will discuss a discharge plan."

Hailey made notes in his electronic record, putting in for the dietary order changes and the tray for Sharla. She also ordered labs to be drawn the following morning. She spoke with the couple a few more minutes, making sure to address questions, then went to check on another patient. Hopefully, Larry Davis would be able to be discharged that day or the following morning.

After disinfecting her hands with the wall sanitizer pump just outside his doorway, Hailey entered the gentleman's room, expecting to see him watching old Westerns as he'd been doing the previous two mornings. Instead, he appeared to be sleeping.

"Good morning, Mr. Davis," she greeted, not wanting to startle him as she approached his bed. His chest was rising and falling, but when he hadn't roused when she reached his bedside, nervousness set in. "Mr. Davis? I'm going to touch your arm."

She placed her hands on his arm and gave a gentle shake. He didn't react to the stimulation. She did a quick pulse check. There, but thready.

"Mr. Davis, this is Dr. Easton. I'm going to listen to your chest," she told him in hope that he was aware of her presence. She placed the diaphragm of her stethoscope on his chest. Grimacing at what she heard, she pulled out her phone to call for assistance.

CHAPTER THREE

"CODE BLUE. CODE BLUE," the announcer blared over Venice General Hospital's PA system then proceeded to give the location of the emergency, citing the medical floor and patient room number. Cayden recognized the number as the one he'd been headed to. Larry Davis had been admitted with sick sinus syndrome earlier in the week and had been improving. He'd been transferred out of the at-full-capacity cardiac care unit to the medical floor two days prior. He'd been somewhat better the previous day and Cayden had planned to recommend he be sent home that day or the next. What had changed?

The man's vital signs, apparently.

Having been in the medical floor hallway, Cayden rushed to Mr. Davis's room, not surprised to see part of the code team in action. That Hailey led the code had his stomach buzzing with excitement the same as it did each time that he saw her. He'd enjoyed their evening together and was looking forward to introducing her to shark tooth hunting. As a friend, he assured himself, despite his attraction to her. Friendship worked with their being coworkers. Being lovers did not. He needed to remember that. You'd think with the beating Cynthia had given his heart he wouldn't need to remind himself. Then again, she hadn't been the first to trample on his affections. Fortunately, she was the last and would remain so as he'd permanently taken his heart off the market.

"Dr. Wilton," Renee said, noticing he had entered the room. While Hailey did chest compressions, the charge nurse delivered oxygen via a bag valve mask.

At his name, Hailey's blue gaze lifted from where she'd been observing Larry, met Cayden's for a millisecond, then returned to her patient, all without her palms pausing from where she rhythmically compressed the man's chest. That brief meeting of their gazes had Cayden sucking in a deep breath before he hit the ground from lack of oxygen himself.

"You want me to take over compressions?" He moved beside her, knowing the lifesaving actions quickly wore out one's arms. Depending upon how long she'd been doing the hundred-plus compressions per minute routine her arms might already be trembling. They'd just called the code, so probably not long, but he wanted to help.

"Either that or you can lead the code until the compression nurse arrives to take this over."

Cayden had been so close he wasn't surprised he'd beat the rest of the code team to the room. His gut instinct told him to let Hailey run the code. Today was her third day on the floor. He'd assist and jump in where needed. He leaned in next to her, clasped his hands, and held them just above Larry's chest. "On the count of three, I'll take over compressions. One. Two. Three." His hands replaced hers in pushing in Larry's chest just over two inches with each downward push. "Fill me in on what happened."

"I came to check him. He looked to be asleep and wouldn't rouse," Hailey told him. "He was breathing, just, but pulse was thready. Systolic blood pressure was in the low sixties. Oxygen saturation was upper seventies then and now."

A nurse rushed in with the crash cart and, while Cayden continued to compress Larry's chest, Renee continued to deliver oxygen via the bag valve mask ventilator. Hailey and the nurse who'd arrived with the supplies dug into the cart, one going for medication while the other opened the defibrillator.

A documenter, security guard, and a respiratory therapist rushed into the room, along with another nurse. The respiratory therapist took over the bag valve mask delivering air. Renee shifted to the crash cart, taking over opening the defibrillator leads and freeing Hailey to assess the situation and direct the code.

A nurse cut Larry's gown out of the way, and Renee pressed the defibrillator leads to the man's chest. Glancing toward the display, Hailey waited the few seconds while the machine assessed Larry's heart's electrical activity.

The defibrillator didn't recommend a shock and Hailey advised, "Keep doing CPR."

"Trade on compressions." The code team's compression nurse leaned in to take over Cayden's role. On the count of three, Cayden shifted back as the nurse immediately started pressing the man's chest.

Stretching out his arms, he stepped back, then moved beside Hailey to assess the situation, his gaze going from the telemetry to the defibrillator's display. The machine screen changed, flashing its new recommendation. She was on top of it, immediately reacting.

"Prepare to deliver shock," Hailey said, then warned, "All clear."

Everyone who'd been administering care stepped back, making sure they weren't touching the patient. First glancing to check that everyone truly appeared all clear, Hailey pushed the button that administered the electrical pulse that would hopefully jolt the patient's heart back into rhythm.

Immediately, Cayden and the others were poised, ready for whatever was needed, all the while holding their breath as they waited for the machine's analysis of Larry's heart rhythm. He was in ventricular tachycardia where his heart was essentially quivering without pumping sufficient blood to supply his body with oxygen.

"Give epinephrine," Hailey ordered, not glancing up as an anesthesiologist entered the room. Good. If the patient warranted intubation, the specialist would be the one to do so. Efficiency of time was of the essence since compression would have to be stopped for tube placement. Cayden could do it, as no doubt could Hailey, but neither of them had the experience the specialist did.

Everyone performing their roles, they continued giving lifesaving measures. As soon as the defibrillator monitor advised to do so, Hailey ordered everyone to step back so she could administer another electrical shock.

"All clear," she said, then pushed the machine's button for a second shock in continued hope of restoring a normal rhythm.

Holding his breath, Cayden watched the screen. There. A normal beat, then another. Another. And another. *Yes.*

"Equipment is showing a normal sinus rhythm," Hailey informed them, her voice calm, but relieved.

A collective sigh went up around the hospital room. Not that Larry was out of the woods, but he was alive, and his heart was currently pumping oxygen out to his body. How long that lasted was another matter. His heart could stay in rhythm or jump right back out. Or worse. His heart could completely stop beating.

"Let's get him ready to transfer to the Cardiac Care Unit," Hailey ordered.

Within minutes, Larry was being transferred to the CCU and would soon thereafter be in the cardiac lab for testing to find out what had triggered his dangerous arrhythmia. Cayden and Hailey traveled down the hallway with the team as they rolled the patient's bed and equipment. Once their patient had been handed off to the CCU, Hailey took a deep breath.

"What a morning, huh?" Cayden asked from where he stood beside her, watching as the CCU team took over Larry's care. "Not even working on the floor a week and you've already saved a man's life. Congratulations."

Hailey gave him a *Yeah, right* look. "Some third day on the job. Not counting orientation, of course." Her gaze going back to their patient, she let out a long sigh.

His heart went out to her. Having a patient to code was never easy. To have one happen so quickly into starting a new job was diving in headfirst. "You did good."

Looking surprised at his compliment, she smiled, but it was a weak one. "Thank you. I'm just glad he didn't die. For so many reasons, that would have been terrible."

"You saved him."

She didn't look convinced, instead shaking her head. "The team saved him."

"The team under your lead," he reminded her, surprised at just how rattled she appeared. Thinking back, he'd probably been rattled on his first few codes, as well.

"Honestly, I was hoping to send him home. I'd thought possibly today." She eyed where the CCU team was setting up Larry's equipment in his new high-intensity care room that was really more of a three-sided area open to the hallway with a large sliding glass door that could be pulled closed for privacy. "Thank goodness I hadn't."

"I'd planned to recommend he go home today, too. The reality is that one's health can change in a heartbeat." He nudged her arm. "Some things can be predicted. Some can't." She knew that but with her so fresh out of residency, he understood why she was being critical of herself. As far as things that could and couldn't be predicted, take his reaction to her, for instance. Because his simple nudge had him intensely aware that he'd touched her. Given where they were, what they'd just experienced, he wouldn't have predicted the zings shooting through him. Yet, there they went. *Zing. Zing. Zing.* He swallowed, then added, "Pun intended, and you have to smile that the heart specialist has jokes."

"Thanks." She smiled and it was a little more real. "The whole team showed up quickly and worked well together. Plus, we had you there. Not every code is lucky enough to have a cardiologist to give a hand." She cut her gaze toward him and surprised him with a nudge of her own, eliciting another flare of zings. "I appreciated you being there, Cayden. To have you and Renee in the room definitely made me feel better just because you were familiar and friendly faces."

Her admission had his stomach flopping. Familiar and friendly. That's what they were destined to be. Not that those zings felt familiar or friendly, but more of an attack on logic and good intentions. "Then I'm glad I arrived when I did. But I have no doubt that you would have been just fine. You ran the code exactly the way I would have done."

Giving an appreciative smile, she stood a little taller and nodded. "You're right. I worked plenty of codes during residency. However, this is my first one while not a resident, the first one at a new hospital, the first one during my first week on the job, and that made it feel different," she admitted, brushing a strayed-from-her-ponytail lock of hair back behind her ear and meeting his gaze. "I'm not sure if that makes sense, but like I said, it was nice knowing I had you there. Is the med-surg floor always this exciting?"

He was glad she'd had him there, too. Not because she'd needed him, but because she'd said his presence had comforted her. He liked that she felt that way, that she'd viewed his presence as a plus. What he wasn't sure of was how much he liked those things or how much he liked the way she was looking at him with more than a little awe mingled in with appreciation.

"Med-surg has it's days, but most are relatively calm compared to the other hospital units." He grinned. "Apparently, despite having never found a four-leaf clover, you're just lucky that way."

She snorted. "The cardiologist really does have jokes. However, that we got him back into rhythm makes me feel lucky." She glanced around the busy CCU room where Larry was being attended to by the nurses, respiratory therapist, and anesthesiologist. "No one wants to lose a patient, but especially not during your first week on a new job." Hesitating a moment, she stared di-

JANICE LYNN   63

rectly into Cayden's eyes, making him feel as if he needed to loosen his collar and his scrub top didn't have one. "I'm no longer needed here and should head back to the medical floor. I've got a few more patients to see for my morning rounds."

She turned to go and had taken a few steps before Cayden caught up to walk beside her. "Me, too. That's why I was so close when the code was called."

She continued toward the elevator bank. "You being so close is something else that makes me feel lucky. Maybe four-leaf clovers are over-rated."

"Maybe." He was glad she seemed to have gotten her composure back and was making jokes. "We should celebrate."

Now where had that come from? They didn't need to celebrate her doing her job. Yet he wanted to take her out to do just that. To celebrate her because his gut instinct said Hailey wasn't used to being celebrated. He probably wasn't the guy who should be doing so, since he was deeply attracted to her physically and they were coworkers. That wasn't a good combination. Just look at the messy situation he'd been in when Cynthia had cheated on him. He'd been ready to promise his future to her and she'd not been faithfully committed to him in the present. Which shouldn't have surprised him. His own parents hadn't been faithful to each other.

Hailey looked at him with confusion. "Celebrate?"

"Life should be celebrated." None of his meanderings of the past made that any less true. "And especially when it's the result of a successful code during one's first work week."

"Ah, I see." Her lips twitched. "In that case, what did you have in mind, Dr. Wilton?"

"Dinner and a toast to the unnecessity of four-leaf clovers for good fortune?"

She hesitated, waiting until they'd reached the elevator bank and she'd pressed the up arrow prior to turning toward him. The elevator door opened. No one was in the car and they stepped inside.

"Dinner two nights in a row?" Her eyes flickered with uncertainty as they met his. "I'm not sure that's a good idea."

Cayden couldn't argue. Somehow, though, he suspected her reasons ran deeper than them working together. "I asked so I'm paying. A free dinner could be called good luck, too."

Her lips twitched, hinting that she was fighting a smile. Good. He wanted to make her smile. "Hasn't anyone ever told you that there's no such thing as a free dinner?"

She was probably right. There was always a

price to be paid, but that didn't keep his insides from lighting up like the Fourth of July when she agreed.

Incoming waves lapped at Hailey's feet as she walked along the shore. She and Cayden had eaten dinner on the same blanket he'd had from the previous night. When they'd finished, she'd said she'd like to walk, and he'd immediately stood. Spending time with a man who didn't purposely do the opposite of whatever she suggested was such an oddity that she'd caught herself staring at him for much longer than she should have. He hadn't seemed to mind, just smiled at her as if it was the most normal thing in the world. The light breeze coming off the water and the temperature felt perfect after a long day spent inside the hospital. The company was perfect, too. Too perfect.

"Tell me about Leanna Moore." What was she doing? Trying to prove to herself that he wasn't perfect? She knew he wasn't. No one was, including and especially her. Or maybe she was trying to sabotage the sense of contentment that being with him filled her with. Contentment? That wasn't the most accurate way to describe how she responded to him. Besides, there was no reason for Cayden to tell her anything about the woman he'd once dated. He and Hailey were just friends...right?

But Cayden didn't seem upset by her inappropriate and out-of-the-blue request. "She and I hit it off for a while. We worked when neither of us was interested in anything long-term. She started wanting something more." He squinted at how the evening sun hit his face. "She's a great person. I was upfront with her that I wouldn't ever want more and we ended the physical side of our friendship before things got too messy for us to remain friends."

Hailey walked closest to the water, and a fresh wave lapped at her feet.

"It's good you remained friends." She and John sure weren't. The unfriendly sentiment was mutual except when he was trying to convince her to return to Ohio. He'd called the night before, but not wanting her enjoyable evening with Cayden spoiled, she'd let the call go to voicemail. "Renee mentioned that you do a weekly segment during her morning radio show."

"I'm flattered that you were talking about me with Renee and curious as to why she would mention Leanna. Not that I go around broadcasting my personal life, but it's no secret that I've been involved with women."

Involved. Hailey mentally gulped at what he

likely meant by that. "Renee must have gotten the wrong impression that you were more serious."

"That we've remained close friends may confuse some." He shrugged. "But, to be fair, at one time Leanna had hoped for a proposal, but that was never going to happen. Not from me. I've no desire to ever get married."

The water pulled back toward the sea, causing the sand to shift beneath Hailey's feet and she fought to keep from stumbling.

"Me, either." Heat infused her cheeks the moment the claim left her lips and she felt compelled to rush on. "Marriage is overrated." Not that she knew firsthand, but by some standards she'd been John's common-law wife due to how long they lived together. Ten wasted years. She wouldn't be risking that again. Relationships never lasted in her life, anyway.

Just as another wave rushed around them, this one climbing midway up Hailey's calf, Cayden stopped walking. "You continue to surprise me, Hailey. Why is it that you agree with my sentiments on marriage?"

"I was in my last relationship for almost a decade." Her *only* relationship. "Between that, school, and residency, I've missed out on a lot in life, you know?" Which was true and easier to admit than going into the details of just how hollow that relationship had been. "I want to do things with friends, the things most people did during their teens and university days, but I didn't. I was too busy making sure I made good grades and working." Next to her, he was quiet, and she wondered if she'd admitted too much. "I'm not sure if that makes sense, but it's where I'm at in my life journey and for the first time in a long time, I feel at peace."

As she said the words, she acknowledged their validity. Not that she'd achieved all or even most of her self-improvement goals, but because she'd taken control of her life and was making steps in the right direction. That she was telling him those things was further validation of how far she'd come. How could he make her so jittery inside and yet be so easy to talk to that she told him things that were so personal? Things that she was just realizing as she was saying them?

"As I said, you surprise me." He met her gaze and she fought to keep from looking away. "Being near the water gives me that sense of peace. I run here most mornings because my day goes better when I've spent time near the water."

Staring into his eyes, she wondered if diving in would bring further peace or throw her into complete turmoil. "If being near the water is what brings peace, then I should have moved long ago."

Concern shone on his face. "I take it your life in Ohio wasn't that great?"

"It led me to here so I'm not going to complain." Because, right here, next to this delicious and kind man who she was pouring her most inner thoughts out to felt like a marvelous place to be. She could tell that he wanted to ask more, but he just nodded. Maybe that was part of why he was so easy to talk to. He seemed to instinctively recognize her comfort zone and didn't push beyond it.

"I'm glad you're here, Hailey." It was probably just how the sun shone, how it hit his gorgeous hazel eyes, how the soft waves lapped at her feet that had her feeling more in sync than she'd ever felt with another person. What was it about him?

"Why?" She couldn't believe she'd asked. Even after all the time they'd lived together, having such an open, honest conversation with John would have been difficult. Impossible even. He hadn't been one for deep conversations. Or conversations at all unless the topic was something that interested him.

"Why not?" Cayden gave a sheepish grin and reached for her hand, entwining his fingers with hers. They were warm, strong, firm, full of electricity that zapped from him to her. Hailey was completely stunned.

Why is he holding my hand?

Heart pounding, she gulped. Taking a deep breath, she reminded herself that she was the new Hailey. The new Hailey could hold a gorgeous man's hand if she wanted to. It didn't mean anything. Maybe this was what friends did. Or maybe he wanted to be more than friends. What was it Renee had said about guarding her heart but still having fun? Being with Cayden was fun. How long had it been since she'd been more than an inconvenience and wallet? Since she'd felt attractive? Wanted? Feminine in all the best ways? Had she ever? When Cayden looked at her, she felt those things. Those scary, wonderful, addictive things.

Why not?

Yeah, she could think of a million reasons, but none of them had her pulling her hand from where it was clasped with his.

Later, orange and red hues painted the sky. Hailey sat on the blanket they had left spread during their walk and Cayden had gone to his car.

"Dessert and our toast to good luck," he proclaimed when he returned, holding up a small bag cooler and wine holder.

She eyed them with mixed feelings. "If I keep hanging out with you, I'm going to gain back the progress I've made in losing weight and will never reach my goal."

His forehead wrinkled. "You're dieting?"

"For my whole life it seems." Mainly, she'd just gotten a bit down after her parents died and the resulting extra pounds had added up over time. Food comforted her, making her feel better in the moment. She didn't like the trait but recognized it as her reality. It was a wonder she hadn't gained a lot more than she had over the last ten years.

Cayden ran his gaze over her, which should have made her want to suck everything in as tightly as she could, but she sat still under his scrutiny.

"The only diet you need is one where you eat healthy."

She snorted. "Says the man who brought appetizers and dessert in addition to the side salad, asparagus, and salmon I ordered for dinner."

"I didn't know I was sabotaging something that was important to you. Fortunately, you're perfect as you are. Besides, I chose fresh strawberries. They're a great source of vitamin C and good for you." He handed her the plastic champagne glasses, then removed the bottle's foil cover.

"No cork?" she asked, having imagined that he'd pop the top. Or was that just something that happened in movies?

"No cork." He grinned mischievously. "You may fault me for a technicality."

Wondering what he meant, she arched a brow. "Uh-oh. What have you done?"

He turned the bottle so that she could read the label.

"Sparkling apple cider?" She tsked as he poured bubbly liquid into one glass and then the other. Why did her insides feel just as bubbly? "You're right. I may deduct points from your celebration skills." Although, not really. She was blown away that he'd brought the bottle.

"I should get an A for effort since I noticed you didn't drink anything alcoholic last night and so I opted for an alternative, just in case." He twisted the top onto the bottle, then slid it back into the cooler bag. She held out one of the plastic glasses. Grinning, he took it, then clinked it to hers. "Here's to your first code's success."

He'd noticed that and adjusted what he'd bought to accommodate what he'd thought she'd want? Gulping back the emotions hitting her, Hailey raised her glass, touching it to his.

"And to points not deducted."

CHAPTER FOUR

ALTHOUGH THEY TEXTED, Hailey didn't see Cayden again until Sunday morning for their planned shark tooth hunt. At least, not outside of her mind, she hadn't. How could she think so much of someone she'd just met? How could she miss him? She'd been off from the hospital on Thursday. It was her designated self-care day. She exercised, got a massage, had her lashes, hair, and nails done on rotation in Sarasota, had her weekly online mental health therapy session, and furniture shopped. She'd not had a lot of things to move as most of her parents' things had been auctioned off after they'd passed. She'd been eighteen and had agreed with what the estate trustee recommended.

With the exception of a few mementoes and a painting of her mother's that John had never liked and insisted stay in the closet, she'd left most things at the apartment she'd shared with him, including the majority of her clothes. She'd wanted very little from her former life, just a few books

and things from school, and had taken off from
Ohio with what fit into her car. Upon arrival,
she'd unpacked at the house she'd bought with
only having seen it online, but knowing it was
the right one. Next, she'd traded her boring sedan
for the shiny blue convertible that had caught
her eye when she'd driven by the lot in Sarasota. Her new life would be filled with things
she'd picked, things she liked, starting with a
bright, airy home, lots of whites and turquoise
colors making up the sea theme she'd chosen.
With initially focusing on her physical appearance and mindset, her new job, and attending
neighborhood events, she'd not had much time
for home decor shopping. When she had gone,
she'd been picky so the process was slow. The
week she'd arrived, she'd bought a bed, chest of
drawers, nightstand, and an oversized amazing
reading chair. She'd made a department store
run for bedding, bath linens, and odd and ends.
The following week, she'd found a four-person
dining room table and chairs to put in the window nook off her kitchen. For a sofa, she'd been
willing to wait until she found just the right one.
Happily, she'd found the one today, along with
a comfy chair, and bleached wooden coffee and
end tables. She made arrangements for the items
to be delivered the following evening, so, despite how she couldn't stop thinking of Cayden,

she'd declined his phoned invitation to listen to a band playing at a nearby community village shopping area.

On Saturday, she went to the cookout with Ryan. He'd been fun, a gentleman, opening the car door and introducing her to his friends. Even though the evening was "just as friends," his attention had made her feel good, but in such a different way from how she felt with Cayden that she'd not been able to prevent comparing the outing with when she was with him. Unfortunately, she'd also not been able to stop wondering what Cayden was doing. Had he gone to listen to music the night before, only with someone as a date rather than friend? Perhaps with Leanna Moore. The green in Hailey's veins didn't bode well for someone who wasn't ready to date and, although innocent and arranged prior to meeting Cayden, was with another man.

Cayden muddied the waters of her somewhat clear vision for her future. She was more attracted to him than she'd known possible. After the horror of her relationship with John, the last thing she should be thinking about was a man. But Cayden was never far from her mind. Had she truly only known him a week?

Was that the real reason she'd not gone with him Friday evening? Fear of how he'd already gotten beneath her skin? After all, she could have invited him to wait with her on her furniture delivery and they could have gone to listen to the music afterward. Was she scared of how he made her feel? And if so, wasn't being afraid letting John still wield control over her life?

On Sunday morning, a beach-adventure-ready Hailey watched for Cayden's arrival and rushed to meet him before he'd much more than gotten out of his car. Her home was still too bare for her to let him in, which didn't make a lot of sense since she'd gotten the new pieces Friday and she'd let Ryan come in when he'd retrieved her for the cookout. It hadn't seemed to matter so much what *he* thought of her bare walls. It shouldn't matter what Cayden thought of her home. It was hers and as long as she loved it, that was what mattered. She didn't have to please anyone else.

"You're very quiet." Cayden glanced her way from the driver's seat of his SUV. As Ryan had, he'd opened the passenger door for her, something John never did. Of course, they'd been very young when they'd first gotten together and that probably made a difference. Maybe. Either way, she'd felt giddy inside like a silly schoolgirl at the gesture. How low were her standards if it took so little to impress her?

Something else to work on—have higher expectations from everyone she let into her life.

"I was thinking about needing to shop for my apartment." The truth, just that she'd had several other thoughts, too. "I've been to several places, but not found what I'm looking for. My walls are very blah." Other than in her bedroom where she had her mother's painting that she cherished. She'd have hung it in her apartment with John if she hadn't feared that he might do something to it if she'd left it in plain sight. "Not that I want clutter, but I hope to find a few special pieces to give the place a splash of me."

"A splash of you?" Cayden chuckled, glancing her way briefly as he maneuvered his vehicle through the light traffic. "That sounds intriguing and possibly painful."

"Ha. Ha. You knew what I meant." She'd wondered how things would be between them with her saying no to going with him Friday. She'd explained about the furniture, but she half expected him to be upset that she'd not done as he wished. His smile and nature were so relaxed that any uncertainty over saying no had quickly dissolved.

As silly as it was since she was similarly dressed, he'd caught her completely off guard with his bare legs as she'd only seen him with scrubs or rolled-up casual slacks. For their shark tooth hunting adventure, he wore a Venice Has Heart T-shirt complete with various local sponsors listed on the back and a pair of yellow with little pink flamingos swim trunks that came to just above his knees. He'd opted for leather sandals. Casual Cayden was just as hot as Dr. Cayden. Maybe more so as he seemed more approachable in his "play" clothes.

More approachable? Ha! If he'd been any more approachable she'd have been pushing him back on the sand after their "celebration" toast and strawberries. That he had a playboy reputation and hadn't made any moves on her should clue her in that, despite his occasional flirty comment and the spark she saw in his eyes that she'd swear was desire, ultimately, he wasn't interested in anything more than friendship.

"What are you needing? Maybe I can help," he offered, fortunately oblivious to her mental ramblings.

"You have spare lamps, pictures, and such lying around to give my house personality?" She didn't know exactly what she wanted, just knew she'd recognize the right additions when she came across them.

"You wouldn't want what's in my house." He tapped his thumbs against the steering wheel. "My condo is the ultimate bachelor pad, right down to the bicycle and surfboard in my living room. But I'm game to changing our plans to going shopping instead of to Caspersen."

Fighting a smile, she eyed him with suspicion. "Afraid you won't be able to live up to your promise of helping me find a shark tooth?"

"I keep my promises." His gaze cut to hers, emphasizing his point with its intensity and having her swallow. "We've plenty of time for finding shark teeth. Just say the word and we'll save that for another time and go shopping today."

That Cayden was willing to change their plans so readily, that he was willing to go shopping with her, had her eyeing him with renewed awe. John would have complained and only have agreed if she'd begged and they'd been shopping for him. He'd do all kinds of things when there was something in it for him.

"I'm not going to be contacted by a home makeover show anytime soon," his grin widened, "but I have decent taste. Plus, having two spare arms to carry things would be helpful."

"Or I could just use a shopping cart," she teased trying not to let her gaze go to where his arms were on display. He looked as if he could carry a lot of things. He wasn't bulky muscled, just really fit, as if he took his role as a cardiologist and promoting good heart health seriously. Hailey swallowed. Yeah, he looked like the poster child—man—for good heart health. Or maybe a poster for a hcartthrob, because he was certainly that, too. Take her heart for instance. It was throbbing so hard that she was surprised it didn't drown out the music he had playing.

He chuckled. "You could, but where's the fun in that?"

"We're not dressed for shopping." She had on her bathing suit beneath her loose shorts and baggy T-shirt. They definitely had a we're-heading-to-the-beach vibe.

"You're in Florida. Beach attire works for most occasions."

She twisted in the passenger seat to more fully look at him. "You would skip going to the beach to go shopping with me?"

He nodded.

"Okay, you may regret this, because I'm going to take you up on your offer." Not that she didn't want to go to the beach with him, but she would like to find a few things for her house and she was curious about shopping with Cayden.

"Just point me in the direction you want to go and that's where I'll drive." He didn't seem the slightest fazed by their change of plans.

"Yeah, that's not a good idea. I'm still learning where things are so you may have to help. Plus, I've searched around here and haven't found what I want. I'm looking for lamps, pictures for my walls, a few cool knickknacks, that kind of thing. As cliché as it may seem, my home theme is the water."

"I'm impressed you have a home theme."

"Other than 'bachelor pad'?" Had she really just batted her lashes when his gaze was on the road, anyway?

"Yeah, I don't see that one working for you." He grinned, then glanced her way. "If you don't mind the drive, there's a place just outside Sarasota that might have what you're looking for."

"I'm good with Sarasota. It's less than an hour and where I purchased my living room furniture." She made the drive every Thursday for her big makeover maintenance.

"To Sarasota it is, then."

Cayden drove her to a large warehouse-type store that offered a variety of new and locally made items. Shopping with him was an adventure. He was funny, made hilarious suggestions, and yet, fairly quickly homed in on her taste preferences. When he pointed out two lamps that had been made by a local artisan, excitement hit.

"Those are amazing." She ran her fingertip over the intricate piece of smooth bleached driftwood that made up the base and neck of one of the lamps. The artist had covered the lower portion of the base with seashells. "Do you think I'm going overboard with my beach theme?"

"You do recall that you didn't let me see your house so I've no basis to answer with any accuracy?"

She gave a sheepish smile. "Sorry."

"But, for whatever its worth, my thought is that if you like the lamps, and you obviously do, buy them." He shrugged. "If, down the road, you decide that you want to change them out, you can. You're not stuck with today's decision forever."

He made a good point and she suspected that she'd regret it if she didn't buy one. She could even envision the piece in her living room next to her new sofa.

"Which do you like best?" She knew which she preferred but was curious if he agreed. Part of her hoped he didn't as he seemed much too in sync with her thoughts.

He ran his gaze over each lamp, then pointed to the one that had originally drawn her attention. "That one. Both pieces are great, but I like how the artist seeped the turquoise into the variances in the wood. It's subtle enough that you barely see it initially, but is a testament to its connection to the sea."

"Sold." Because, seriously, how could she not choose that one since he'd picked the lamp she'd liked best? Or ever get rid of the piece when he'd described the design exactly how she'd seen it? The subtle hint of color inflected into the wood added just the right pizzazz. She suspected she'd never look at it without being reminded of him, which gave her a moment's pause. She didn't want her home to remind her of him or anyone. It was supposed to be about her, her safe place and haven from the world. Still, she had chosen prior to his description and truly, the lamp was perfect. "Let's put those 'spare arms' to use."

Grinning, he picked up the lamp. "While you finish looking, I'll take this to the cashier for them to hold until we're ready to check out."

Hailey didn't find anything else that jumped out at the shop, but she loved the lamp and paid for it. Cayden loaded the artsy light onto the back floorboard of his SUV. He placed the shade on the seat, then used the towels he'd brought for their beach excursion to protectively place around the lamp.

"I could sit back there and make sure it doesn't get banged around," she offered. Truth was, she was impressed by his thoughtfulness in how he arranged the lamp.

"And have me looking like I'm driving Miss Hailey?" He wrinkled his nose. After one last check to make sure the lamp was secure, he got into the driver's seat. "I prefer to have you up here next to me." He buckled his safety belt, then started the car. "Are you in a hurry?"

"Not necessarily. What do you have in mind?"

"The bigger farmers markets are on Saturday but there are some that carry over onto Sundays.

They usually have a variety of vendors ranging from food to artisans. There's one not too far from here," he told her. "We could grab lunch, walk around to see if we can find any other treasures for your home."

Her home. Not her apartment, but her home. Because that was what she was making in Florida. A home for herself.

A home and a new life that she liked more and more.

A couple of hours later, Cayden watched as Hailey surveyed the ice cream selection with eyes as big as any child's. Rather than order, she turned to him and shook her head.

"I'm going to pass. Thanks, though."

"It's organic and made with all-natural ingredients," he said. They'd eaten a healthy lunch and he'd been the one to suggest ice cream. Ice cream was his weakness. Not that he did, but he could eat it every single day and not get tired of the cold dessert. He wasn't even picky on what flavor. He liked them all. Some better than others. In his book, there were no bad ice cream flavors.

"That's not it. You go ahead."

Then he remembered she'd mentioned dieting. How did he convince her that her curves were perfect without making her self-conscious or have her to think he was being a jerk? Because he really liked the ease in which they'd enjoyed their day and didn't want to do anything that jeopardized that comradery. It had been a good day. A great day. Surely, she must think so, too.

Sure, he'd been a bit prickly Friday evening when they'd been on the phone and she'd said she had to wait on her furniture. Her reason had felt as flat as if she'd said she had to wash her hair. That he'd been disappointed had bothered him. He had no right to be bothered that she'd said no, but he'd spent most of his on call day mulling over just how much it had.

He didn't want more than friendship with her, and yet…he did. Hailey was refreshing, with an air of innocence mingled with an irresistible feminine allure that sucked him right in.

"I'm not eating ice cream if you're not, Hailey." He would be a jerk if he did that when he knew she wanted ice cream, too. But he didn't want her to feel he was sabotaging her if he pushed. He wanted her happy with herself. If she could see herself as he saw her, she would be. He'd hoped that with their plans being to go to the beach that she'd have foregone the makeup, because he longed to see her without it, but she'd been fully made up. He knew she was just as stunning barefaced as she was with all the latest beauty aids. How much he longed to see what she didn't readily reveal to the world should have Cynthia's name flashing through his mind like a warning beacon, but instead was muffled by how protective he felt at Hailey's vulnerability. He suspected someone had done a real number on her body image and although it wasn't Cayden's place to clear her vision to her true beauty, he wanted to do just that. Seeing how she still longingly stared at the display, he suggested, "How about if I order a small bowl and share a few bites?"

"I—" She glanced toward him, a slow smile spreading across her lovely mouth. "Okay, but just a few bites."

That a girl. "Which flavor do you want?"

She pointed to his favorite and he grinned. Incredible how in tune they were. "Great choice."

He ordered two scoops in a small bowl, then paid the cashier while another employee prepared their order. He slid his money clip into his pocket and took the ice cream bowl. Hailey had walked over to where a wide ledge served as a bar top–style table at the base of the storefront window. She sat on a stool and stared out at the boardwalk. Yeah, she should see what he saw. She was so beautiful she stole his breath and yet, it was the pureness in her eyes, in how she looked through the glass with appreciation of everything she was seeing, in how she smiled when she glanced up and saw him. That sweet, genuinely-happy-he'd-bought-ice-cream smile got him right in the feels.

"Remember, this is guilt-free ice cream." He pulled one of the spoons from the ice cream and handed it to her. "Enjoy."

"I didn't see 'guilt-free' written anywhere in the description."

"It should have been. For real, this place is known for using all-natural ingredients, nothing GMO or processed." He pulled the other spoon from the ice cream, a large glob sticking to the utensil. He stuck the cold confection in his mouth and savored the fruity flavor. "Mmm. Good and good for you."

"Next thing, you'll be trying to sell me ocean-front property in Arizona." Watching him, Hailey toyed with her spoon. "It's not fair that men can eat whatever they want and still look like you."

He scooped a second bite. "That's not an accurate statement."

"Do you eat whatever you want?" she challenged, still not using her spoon for anything other than to point it toward him.

Fortunately, other than his ice cream addiction, he ate a healthy Mediterranean diet and was lucky that he preferred eating clean. Ice cream was his guilty pleasure, and even then, he sought ones made with natural ingredients.

"I exercise regularly," he defended.

"No doubt."

Her tone made him smile and he flexed a little. "You like these?"

Snorting, she rolled her eyes with great exaggeration. "It's mostly your modesty that impresses me."

"I get that a lot." Laughing, he gestured to the bowl. "Eat up before it melts and you have a strawberry milkshake instead of ice cream."

Hailey ate one bite to his every three, and her bites were tiny in comparison to his, but at least she did eat some of the dessert and seemed to savor each bite. He refrained from saying anything more for fear she'd stop eating altogether. He didn't want to be a stumbling block, but whoever had made her think she needed to diet deserved a hardy talking to.

When they'd finished their dessert, they headed back out onto the blocked-off street where numerous vendors were selling their wares. The smell of roasted cinnamon pecans and almonds from a nearby booth filled the air and lured several passersby.

"Admit it," he said, glancing toward where she was taking in the busy booths and their various goods. "The ice cream was worth it."

"Sure, it was." Amused sarcasm laced her words. "At the moment," she added. "However, if you ask me when I'm in the gym huffing and puffing and it takes me more than an hour to burn off what I just ate…" She let her voice trail off, then clicked her tongue. "I really shouldn't have."

"You know you look fabulous, right?"

Her cheeks went bright pink. "Thank you for saying so, but I'm well aware that I've always been a little pudgy. I gained extra weight on top of that during med school. I want to get it back off. I've lost some since completing residency and I plan to keep working on the rest. I don't fool myself that I'll ever be thin, but I'd like to be healthy, you know?"

He ran his gaze over her and shook his head. "What you call pudgy, I call sexy."

"And my ex called fat." Her color heightened after her words slipped out, letting him know she hadn't meant to say them.

Right in the middle of the busy-with-pedestrians street, he stopped walking to look directly at her, letting the crowd weave around them. "For the record, your ex was an idiot."

Looking stunned, Hailey's blue eyes lifted to his, then her mouth slowly curved upward. "You're right. He was."

That smile… She obviously had no clue how seductive her mouth was, how the curve of her neck should be listed as lethal to a man's peace of mind because he was so wanted to nuzzle her there. How—*get yourself together*, he ordered. Where were they…oh, yeah.

"Good, we're in agreement. Don't let his lack of good sense influence how you see yourself. You're beautiful. Inside and out. Now, let's go check out those paintings at that booth just up ahead." With that, he grabbed her hand, lacing his fingers with hers, and took off walking as if it weren't a big deal that he was holding her hand.

But, just as when they'd been walking on the beach, Hailey's soft hand clasped within his felt as if touching her was a very big deal. Even more so than during their sunset stroll. Which meant he probably shouldn't be holding her hand. But he wasn't letting go.

Not when Hailey held on to his hand as if he'd offered her a lifeline to lift her from some terrible place she'd been stuck for much too long.

"I love it!" Hailey exclaimed of the artwork Cayden had just hung on her living room wall. She'd been anxious about letting him inside her house, wondering what he'd think of what she'd done thus far. As he'd been helping her carry her purchases inside, she'd not had much choice short of turning him away at the door. The truth was, she'd enjoyed their day, enjoyed being with him. And, as nervous as she'd thought she'd be at his seeing her incompletely put together house, when he'd walked in, he'd glanced around and that he'd liked what he'd seen was obvious.

His approval shouldn't matter. She'd lived on edge trying to get John's approval. She sure didn't want to be in a relationship where that misery became part of her day-to-day existence again. A big difference, she reminded herself, was that no matter what she did, John never really gave his approval regarding anything that wasn't to his benefit. Cayden seemed to selflessly give his time and again. That made her smile big. How wonderful to be with someone who made you feel better about yourself?

With his hands resting on his hips, he stared at her new picture. "She's growing on me."

"Ha! Don't give me that. You were the one to point her out to me." Pulling her gaze from him, Hailey admired the mermaid with her soulful eyes, turquoise tendrils and tail, and the chaotic sea. Wild waves crashed about the mermaid, but she appeared at ease, her expression one of being at peace with the world. The artist had used broken shells to create the mixed media rock emerging from the sea that the mermaid perched upon and nacre to make a pearly bikini top. Hailey had immediately fallen in love with the piece and how well it would look with her living room decor. She'd been right.

"You thought that meant I liked her?" He clicked his tongue. "I was joking when I said you should buy her."

Unfazed by his ragging, she shook her head. "No, you weren't. You like her as much as I do." His poor attempt to look innocent of her accusation failed miserably. "That's why you insisted upon buying her as a housewarming gift," she reminded him, still stunned by his generosity after a lifetime of only gifts from her parents. John had come through with holiday gifts, but they'd always been generic types of things. Supermarket flowers on her birthday. A small box of chocolates on Valentine's. New department store gloves and scarf set at Christmas year after year. Thank God she had no need of his gloves and scarfs in Florida. She'd left them all. Not that there would have been anything wrong with his gifts if they'd come with feeling rather than an obligatory holiday appeasement and expectation that she'd have done something extravagant for him. Besides, how many gloves and scarf sets had she needed? None now, because she had finally stepped into the sunshine. She met his gaze and hoped he could see how much she appreciated him. "Thank you, again, Cayden."

His brow lifted, but after a moment in which he looked torn on what he might say, he returned his attention to the artwork. "There is something about her that latches on to you and won't let go, isn't there? And you're welcome. I'm glad you gave in to my gifting her to you."

She hadn't wanted to, but he'd insisted that he'd spotted the artwork first and called dibs, saying that it was the perfect housewarming gift for a friend who'd just moved to town. He was smooth with the lines. Yet she didn't doubt his sincerity or that she would always treasure the piece. "Even the colors are perfect. As if she was meant to come home with me."

He gestured to where she'd put her new lamp. "That looks great, like it was made for this room, too. Great find."

"You're an expert at this shopping thing, too." He really was, and she'd had tons of fun in the process. "Maybe instead of shark tooth hunting, we can look for big shells. I'd like to have one to put on the table there."

He looked at her in question. "A conch shell?"

She nodded. "I think that's what they're called."

"You don't need to buy one. We can find good shells around here, but if we don't find what you're looking for, then we can go to Sanibel Island."

Sanibel Island. She'd heard of it at some point but couldn't place where it was in her mind. "How far away is that?"

He shrugged. "Just a couple of hours drive."

She gave a horrified look. "A couple of hours is too far to drive to find a seashell."

He laughed. "Where's your adventurous spirit?"

"Hidden beneath my practicality that says driving a couple of hours to find a seashell doesn't make good common sense. Especially when there are dozens of tourist shops around here that sell shells."

"We could say that we're going to Sanibel Island for sightseeing, rather than for shell hunting. Or maybe we will find one when we go shark tooth hunting. The catch to finding great ones really is to either go early or to dive to find them, though."

She adjusted where the lamp sat on the end table. Happiness bubbled inside. The lamp and the painting truly were the perfect finds and she'd had the most perfect day. "Dive?"

"Snorkeling," he clarified. "Although, we could scuba, too. Truthfully, if you were game to learn, that would be the best way to find what you want."

She shook her head. She could wait on finding a shell. There was no rush. "Ohio girl, remember? I'm not used to the ocean. I'd never been prior to moving here and the idea of snorkeling or diving makes me feel claustrophobic."

He looked taken aback. "You moved here

without ever having visited? Where was your practicality when you made that decision?" His teasing tone filtered out any real judgment in his question.

"It seemed like a good idea at the time." Glancing around her bright, airy house, which made her feel free and light by just being in it, then at him, she lowered her lashes and smiled. "It's early yet, but so far, I'd say moving here was a great idea."

His eyes crinkled with his return smile. "You're liking our subtropical climate and good-natured natives, eh?"

"Absolutely." Everyone she'd met had been kind, especially him. That he was also the hottest man she'd ever met…she fought fanning her face. "The sunsets are beautiful, too."

"Some say they're spectacular."

Had he just stepped closer? Oh, heaven above, she really was about to fan her face.

"Speaking of sunsets, last night's was amazing. Did you see it?" he asked.

"Not really," she admitted. "I was at a cookout with a friend, and after eating, we were playing games in a small fenced-in backyard where the view wasn't that great so I didn't pay much attention."

An odd look settled onto his face as his gaze met hers. "A male friend?"

"Yes. A neighbor offered to introduce me to his friend group. They were a fun bunch. You'd like them."

The cookout, meeting Ryan's friends, playing cornhole, terrible as she'd been, had been fun. She'd been a little giddy that she was checking another box of having her new life.

"Are you going to see this neighbor again?" Cayden's eyes darkened and even though the evening had been innocent, she had trouble holding his gaze. She took a step back.

"I'm sure I will." She'd bumped into Ryan each time she'd gone to the community room events and he was frequently in the workout room while she was there for her early morning torture sessions. He'd been sweet and she'd enjoyed meeting his friends. They hadn't made any specific plans, but he'd asked if it was okay to call, and she'd said it was. Making friends was a priority and Ryan was one of the first she'd met.

"Oh." Cayden's face blanched of color, then red splotched his cheeks.

His "oh" held so much disappointment and negativity that she couldn't let it pass. She'd dealt with both much too often. Fingers curling into her palms, she said, "Go on."

"What do you want me to say, Hailey? That I'm glad that you went out with this guy last night and that you're planning to see him again?" He harrumphed. "I can't do that."

"Ryan," she supplied prior to thinking better of it.

"That's his name?" Cayden asked. She nodded, and he continued, "Okay, you told me to go on, so I will." He flexed his jaw. "I'd rather you not go out with Ryan again."

She fought flinching. John telling her what she could and couldn't do echoed through her mind. He wouldn't have said "rather you not" but would have just told her that she wasn't going to. That didn't seem to matter though as she lifted her chin.

"The cookout was just as friends, but for the record, you don't get a say in whether or not I go on a date with someone." Even as she said it, she questioned the validity of her bravado. Disappointing Cayden bothered her. She didn't want to disappoint him and that irked. She'd spent ten years trying not to disappoint John. Ten years that she'd never get back. She needed to focus on not disappointing herself and not another man.

"It's just—" Cayden stopped, raked his fingers through his hair, and closed his eyes as if he was at a loss for words.

"Just what?" Barely able to breathe, she crossed her arms and stared at him.

"The truth is that I'm jealous you were with

another man last night, Hailey." He appeared as shocked as she was by his confession. Shocked, and perhaps a bit self-disgusted. "How's that for a truthful admission?"

Hailey's knees threatened to give way. "Why would you be jealous?"

"I like you." He didn't sound thrilled by his admission, but he'd said the words without hesitation.

Her heart pounded. She was standing in her living room, staring at the most gorgeous man she'd ever known, and he'd just said he liked her. Was this what it felt like to have the most popular guy in school notice you when you were of the wallflower variety?

"I like you, too."

Cayden's gaze didn't waver from hers. "Yet you were with another man last night? Why would you do that?"

She hadn't done anything wrong. His questions made her feel like bringing up all kinds of protective walls. Her evening had just been "as friends," but if it had been a date, she was well within her rights to have gone. She was not wrong to want to experience life.

"I just met you this past week," she reminded him, trying to choose her words wisely because she didn't want to argue with Cayden. How surreal was it that she felt as if she'd known him much longer? In reality, she'd been to the beach with him twice, seen him at work, and spent today with him. They were strangers. And yet, they weren't. She felt as if she knew him better than the man she'd lived with for almost ten years. "I can't even believe we're having this conversation."

"You're right." Frowning, he worked his jaw from one side then to the other. "Does *Ryan* know about me?"

Stunned, Hailey stared at him. "Why would I have told Ryan about you? A week ago today, he invited me to the cookout so I could get to know people because I'm new in town. You and I are coworkers." She put her fisted hands on her hips. "Please explain why Ryan would need to know anything about you?"

Cayden stared at the woman glaring at him and thought her well within her right to do so. Everything she said was true. What was wrong with him? He was acting like a jealous boyfriend.

He didn't do boyfriend. Hadn't in years. Sure, he'd gone out, but he'd only been involved with women who knew the score and didn't have false expectations. He'd let his romantic involvement with Leanna go on too long as she'd started wanting more and losing their friendship would have been a shame. Cynthia had been his last real girlfriend where his heart had been involved and, after that had ended as disastrously as his previous attempts at being in a supposedly committed relationship, he'd given up on happy-ever-after and was quite content with his happy-right-now status. Why he'd ever thought such a mythical thing existed was beyond him. It sure hadn't been the example his parents had set. Great as they were individually, together they'd been malignant. As far as jealous? Yeah, he didn't do that, either. Why had he told Hailey he was jealous?

Because it was true. Right or wrong, for the first time in forever the thought of a woman being with anyone other than him had him seeing green.

"You're right." Because what else could he say?

Her jaw dropped. "I am? I mean, of course, I am. I'm just surprised that you're admitting it. That's a new one for me."

"I've said it before, but your ex was an idiot." He paced across the room, staring at her mixed-media mermaid and battling emotions that felt as tumultuous as the artwork's churning sea. "That you were out with another man last night caught me off guard, Hailey. That's all."

He couldn't call it cheating because that implied something existed between him and Hailey that didn't. But he couldn't squelch his dislike of the idea of her with another man, even if only as friends. Years had passed since the last time he'd cared about what a woman did with her time away from him. He wasn't the jealous type. Yet he wanted to beat his chest and warn this Ryan guy to stay away.

What's wrong with me?

"Am I missing something, Cayden?" Hailey pushed.

He turned back, taking in the stubborn tilt to her chin, the just as determined glint in her eyes. How was he supposed to explain that he didn't want a relationship, but he didn't want her out with other men? He couldn't tell her that. She'd laugh in his face or tell him to get out or both. Rightly so.

"Cayden?" She came to stand a foot in front of him when he remained silent. "We had such a great day. I don't want to argue with you. I don't understand what's happening."

What was happening was that his gaze had dropped to her mouth, watching as her lips formed each word, and now, all he could think, feel, was how much he wanted to kiss her. Out of desire, but also, as a way of staking his claim.

Frustrated with himself, he shook his head. "Nothing. I just—it's time I go."

Because as easy as it would be to give in to

what he wanted to do, to kiss her, how strongly that he didn't want anyone else doing the same, made his head spin. He did not want to stake a claim. He didn't care what women did when they weren't with him. He hadn't since he'd found out Cynthia had been screwing around with another man. Beyond that, hadn't he decided that he and Hailey were coworkers, and anything more than friendship would be complicated?

Friendship with Hailey was already complicated.

Even so, unable to resist, he leaned in, and kissed her forehead. "Good night, Hailey."

With that, he hightailed it out of her house. Denying just how much Hailey got under his skin had become impossible. That quick peck to her forehead had done little to appease the culminating burn within him.

Since she claimed to not want marriage any more than he did, and he saw how she looked at him, sometimes so innocently that he wasn't even sure if she was aware how hot desire burned in her eyes, maybe he shouldn't deny either of them.

But if they became lovers, could they remain friends after the fires died down?

He liked Hailey more than as just the woman he wanted to devour from head to toe. They may have only known each other for a week as she'd so sassily pointed out, but he was positive he'd miss her if he lost her friendship.

CHAPTER FIVE

"GOOD MORNING," a tired Hailey greeted Melvin Little and his wife the following morning. Mondays had always been just another day as during residency she was just as likely to work on weekends as weekdays. More so, usually. With her new Monday through Wednesday work schedule, she rotated out with other physicians and would cover one weekend a month. Had she not tossed and turned all night with thoughts of Cayden, of trying to figure out what that little kiss had meant and why he'd left, then she might feel rested. Instead, she'd used drops to try to clear her red eyes and applied extra powder to hide her dark circles. Maybe no one would notice. She smiled a little brighter at her patient. "I hoped you'd be recovered enough that you'd have been dismissed prior to my returning to work this morning."

The bushy white-haired man scooted up in his hospital bed, grimacing a little as he did so, but moving easier than he had the last time she'd examined him. "Hoping to not have to see me again, Doc?"

She shook her head. "Just wishing you well." She glanced at the blanket in Sharla's lap. "Wow. You've gotten a lot of your afghan completed. That's wonderful."

"Thank you." Keeping a tight hold on her needle and yarn, Sharla proudly held up the sunset-colored piece. "I'll probably have it finished within the next couple of days if he doesn't go home."

"Is that a request to keep him here until you've finished?" Hailey teased, running her hand beneath a hand sanitizer dispenser, then moving beside where Melvin lay. He still appeared pale, but his color was better.

"Could you?" Laughing, Sharla shot her husband a loving look. "When I get him home, he's going to be his usual cantankerous self and thinking I'm supposed to wait on him hand and foot. Having him here is like a vacation for me."

Melvin grunted at his wife's poking. "Don't let her fool you. She lives to dote on me. She did the same with the kids and now the grandkids. They came by yesterday. The whole lot of them. This room was a madhouse for an hour or so. Be glad you missed the chaos."

Hailey couldn't imagine having a big family and what it must feel like to have them be there for you. Those too-short years she'd had with the Eastons had just given her a taste of family life and then it had been ripped away.

She cleared her throat and her thoughts. "That's good you got to see them, but I hope you didn't overdo it."

He shrugged. "Hard to overdo anything when I'm just lying in a hospital bed and waiting on this old body to heal."

"There are different ways to overdo it." After first gloving up, Hailey listened to his heart, his lungs, then checked his abdomen. Everything sounded, looked, and felt as it should other than his chronic heart issues. He seemed to be improving from his surgical emergency and was slowly getting his strength back. "I think I have bad news for you, Sharla. His white blood cell count was completely normal this morning. His surgical site is healing with no redness, drainage, or other sign of infection from his ruptured appendix. His BNP, that stands for brain natriuretic peptide, is still elevated, but not so elevated that home management of his heart failure shouldn't be sufficient. His numbers may have come down enough to be at his baseline, even. But either way, the levels are safe to further address in an outpatient setting. Dr. Wilton—" her heart squeezed as she said his name out loud "—will be by this morning and will be able to give you more information regarding your outpatient heart failure follow-up. As long as he's in agreement, then you'll be discharged later today."

"That's wonderful." Sharla smiled at her husband.

"Doc, that's the best news I've heard since I showed up at this place," Melvin said, coughing as he did so.

Hailey hadn't heard any rattles in his chest, nor had his chest X-ray picked up on any fluid buildup in his lungs. His cough and continued elevated BNP concerned her, but when everything was overall so improved, those weren't sufficient reasons to maintain acute inpatient care.

She talked with the couple a few more minutes, then left his room to round on the remainder of her patients. The unit was full, but no one had anything too exciting going on. When Hailey returned to the office cubicle behind the nurses' station to make further chart notations, Renee glanced up from where she worked and grinned big.

"You just missed Dr. Wilton." The nurse manager eyed Hailey curiously as if she was expecting a reaction. Hailey did her best not to give one as Renee continued, "I think he was going to Room 211." Renee waggled her drawn-on brows. "If you hurry, you can catch him."

Catch Cayden. Hailey's heart sped up. She

hadn't been able to quit thinking of him the night before. Mostly, she marveled that he liked her enough that he was upset that she had gone to the cookout with Ryan and had admitted that he was jealous. Even with the hair color, extensions, weight loss, and the rest of her big makeover, how was that even possible?

Struggling to hide how knowing he was near affected her, Hailey adjusted her stethoscope from where the tubing poked up from her scrub top's pocket. "Did he need to consult with me on a patient?"

Hopefully oblivious to the thundering in Hailey's chest, Renee shook her head. "Not that I'm aware of. I was just letting you know that he came by so that, you know, you could find a reason to bump into him, talk to him, maybe mention sharing dinner and another romantic sunset with him. That kind of thing."

"Not once have I said I shared a romantic sunset with Dr. Wilton." Not out loud, but they had been romantic. *Spectacular.* "Nor is there a reason for me to purposely bump into him, Renee." No reason other than she yearned to see him, to know if he was upset with her, to know if frustration would still shine in his gorgeous eyes when he looked at her. Maybe she didn't want to see him, because if he gave her a cold shoulder, how was she going to hide her disappointment? Why would he give her a cold shoulder when he'd kissed her good-night? A peck, but it had been a kiss. Plus, he'd said he was jealous. That had to mean something.

What do I want it to mean?

"Did he make any notes on Mr. Little? I'm planning to discharge him today unless Dr. Wilton prefers he be kept one more night for further observation."

"He hasn't yet." Renee gave a sly grin that hinted she wasn't buying Hailey's lack of forthcoming details. Her coworker would have a field day if she knew Hailey had seen him outside of work two additional times since their Manasota sunset and that Cayden's lips had touched her the night before. Her forehead. But they had touched her. Perhaps her coworker could see the scorch marks, because she was fairly positive her skin was branded from the simple caress. "He's in with Mr. Little now."

Hailey's belly churned. How would Cayden act around her? Would he be friendly or standoffish? If the latter, would it be from being professional or as a carryover from his displeasure at her having gone to the cookout with Ryan? Whatever Cayden's reaction, he'd be professional. He wouldn't cause a scene or purposely trigger hospital gossip.

"Oh, goody. You don't have to not purposely

bump into him, because there he is now." Renee gestured to behind where Hailey stood. "Hello, Dr. Wilton. Your timing is perfect. Look who is back at the nurses' station."

Yeah, Cayden was professional and wouldn't cause hospital gossip. Renee, on the other hand, had no issue with saying whatever popped into her mind. Despite her warnings to guard her heart, her coworker had completely gotten on board with the idea of Cayden and Hailey. Maybe because she considered herself the cupid who had shot the arrow and felt invested in their relationship. Either way, Hailey believed Renee's intentions weren't malicious, but, oh, how she wished she wouldn't be so obvious.

Taking a quick breath, Hailey turned, met Cayden's gaze and attempted to read his mood. Instantly, she realized that he was doing the same. Had he been concerned that she'd be upset with him? In the entirety of their relationship, John had never cared if he'd upset her. If he had, she'd been expected to get over it and to not do whatever had caused him to upset her again. Even with his cheating, he'd blamed her, citing that she had been too distracted with medical school and residency to meet his needs.

Why did I forgive him time and again?

Swallowing at her own past follies, she smiled at Cayden and after only a moment's hesitation, his lips curved upward, too. Hailey's entire body lightened as her muscles released from the tension that had bound them.

No matter what happened, she wanted to end up as friends with Cayden. Maybe that's all they should be to preserve that future friendship and their working relationship. But how could she insist upon something that she wasn't sure she could do? Because the bubbles of giddiness filling her at his smile weren't bubbles of just wanting to be his friend.

"Good morning, Dr. Wilton." She kept it more formal for Renee's benefit, but knew he'd know why she had. He wore his standard hospital navy scrubs that pulled out the golden flecks in his hazel eyes and she had to fight the strong urge to hug him because he'd so readily smiled back. He didn't seem to play the games she'd come to expect.

Do not put him on a pedestal. You've only known him a week, she reminded herself.

Why did it feel as if she'd known him on some level her entire existence? Thinking she'd lost her mind, she cleared her throat. "What are your thoughts on Mr. Little?"

"He has high hopes of going home today." Cayden grasped the tip of the stethoscope he had draped around his neck, the muscles in his arms flexing as he did so and drawing Hailey's gaze.

His teasing flashed through her mind and her belly clenched at the memory. It was too late to think of Cayden as just a friend. Maybe at some point in the future she'd be able to, but the man tangled up her nerve endings into a hormonal mess she hadn't known she was capable of being.

The real question was what was she going to do about how he affected her? He didn't want anything serious. She didn't want anything serious. Why couldn't they just have fun together? Why couldn't he truly impart some of his expert advice to guide her through her initial "dating" debut? She wanted to explore the joy he triggered within her, to flirt and revel in his attention for however long it lasted. As long as she kept her heart safely tucked away, what would be wrong with soaking up the deliciousness of time spent with him?

Biting into her lower lip, Hailey forced her gaze back to his face, realized Cayden knew exactly what she'd looked at, thought, and she gulped. "Are you on board with his being discharged today?"

Okay, so her voice might have been a slightly higher pitch than normal, but for the most part she'd managed to sound professional.

"His heart failure is chronic, stable overall, and had nothing to do with his initial admission. His surgical complications from his ruptured appendix are resolving." Cayden's gaze stayed connected to hers to the point where Hailey felt the conversation was something personal rather than purely professional, that there were two conversations occurring. One with words and another with their eyes. "From an acute cardiac standpoint, Melvin is safe to go home and will definitely be more comfortable there while he recuperates. His wife will keep close tabs and will get him back here if anything changes."

"Absolutely," she agreed, grateful his assessment had been the same as hers and even more grateful that he seemed as relieved that everything was okay between them as she was. They'd talk soon, away from the hospital. She'd figure out how to say she wanted to spend time with him, to date him, even. But that she would date other men, too, if the opportunity and desire to presented itself. The new Hailey wouldn't be bound by an exclusive relationship that could a man power to dictate her life the way John had. She wouldn't risk getting too close to Cayden and falling into old habits. Seeing other men would be a constant reminder not to get too attached because she and Cayden were casual. "I'll write up discharge orders and have a hospital follow-up appointment scheduled with his primary care provider. Do you want to see him in your office in a few days, as well? Or to just have him follow up with you at his regularly scheduled cardiac checkup?"

"Within the next two weeks would be best."

I'm sorry about last night. That's what his eyes were saying, what her heart was hearing.

"Have my office get him worked in on my schedule."

Me, too, she told him back.

At least she hoped her eyes were broadcasting as clearly as his were. Were hers also transmitting the hesitation she saw in his? He wasn't his usual, teasing self, making reading him difficult and she was far from an expert at her best moments.

"I'll get it noted." Listen to them sounding all business. Standing there, staring at each other, Renee watching them with a Cheshire cat grin, Hailey felt self-conscious because she wasn't sure what to say or do with their audience. She looked at the charge nurse. "What?"

"Nothing." But Renee was smiling when she turned back to her computer screen. When the charge nurse started humming, Hailey shook her head and gave Cayden a *Sorry...* look.

"Don't forget that this Thursday evening is a meeting regarding the Venice Has Heart event," Cayden continued. "It's at six in the Main Street Community Room. I hope you're planning to be there."

"Of course." Avoiding looking directly toward Renee in case her coworker glanced up, Hailey nodded. No way would she be able to hide her thoughts if she met Renee's gaze. "Thursday works perfectly as I'm off from the hospital. I truly do want to get involved in community events and to be helpful wherever I can. I planned to volunteer with some charities even before I moved to Florida. I feel lucky to have done so this quickly thanks to Renee."

"That's great. We appreciate everyone who volunteers." Yeah, she doubted their conversation was fooling Renee.

"I'm looking forward to meeting the other volunteers." She was. Making friends was high on her priority list for her big move to Florida. She'd been so isolated for so long. She was getting to know some of her neighbors via their HOA neighborhood activities and community gym, and she'd met Ryan's group at the cookout. Slowly, but surely, she'd make friends.

"We have the best volunteers at Venice Has Heart. I..." He hesitated then seemed to change his mind about whatever he'd considered saying. She assumed that Renee being able and eager to hear their discussion limited what he was saying as it did for Hailey.

There was a quiet pause where they just looked at each other, then Hailey gave a nervous laugh.

"I should get Mr. Little's discharge started. He'll be excited that you're in agreement for him to go home. Sharla is going to have her hands full."

She'd hoped he'd say something more, but after a moment of obvious debating with himself that had Renee looking back and forth between them, he just nodded. "Sounds good, Hailey. Thanks for taking care of that."

She didn't see him again that day and considered texting him, but decided she shouldn't. No matter how many self-confidence podcasts she listened to while doing household chores and therapy sessions she attended, she wasn't sure she'd ever get over her insecurities. What if Cayden had realized he wasn't interested in anything more than friendship and being her co-worker? Either way, she'd be fine, she assured herself. She did not need him or any man for affirmation of her value. She was enough. Just ask her therapist.

After work, Hailey stopped by a home goods store and purchased an outdoor patio set that included a propane-fueled fire pit and arranged to have it delivered early Thursday as she didn't have any self-care appointments until later in the day. She found an outdoor rug that matched and managed to finagle it into her new car by lowering the convertible top and buckling it into the passenger seat. If she envisioned having friends to come over to visit, socializing with them while sitting on her patio, it would happen, right?

The following two days, one of Cayden's partners was on call for the cardiology rounds. In his late forties, Dr. Brothers was polite, to the point, and there and gone in under fifteen minutes each morning. Having known the posted call schedule didn't keep Hailey from feeling disappointed as each day passed without her seeing or hearing from Cayden. On Wednesday evening, she started a yoga class and ended up with a coffee date for the following morning with another newcomer who worked as a nurse at an extended living facility.

After an hour at her community gym and her patio furniture delivery, she met Jamie, and had a low-carb protein smoothie that tasted pretty good. They ended up walking around the man-made lake near the shopping center, chatting away as they continued to get to know each other. Jamie had recently moved to the area and was as eager to make friends as Hailey. They promised to make their Thursday mornings a new tradition. Hailey would have to adjust the timing on her Sarasota beauty session trips, but that should be easy enough by planning ahead.

That evening, Hailey debated on what one would wear to a Venice Has Heart volunteer meeting. She ended up settling on a casual

power-red skirt, white eyelet top, and comfy sandals from her new wardrobe. Not too casual and
not too dressy.

When she arrived at the community center,
she wasn't sure where to go, but met up with a
very tan and fit late sixties couple. They claimed
to be longtime volunteers and advised her to follow them. They were dressed casually in shorts,
T-shirts, and sandals so she was glad she'd not
chosen anything dressier. When they entered
the room, there were already around thirty volunteers present, including Cayden and Leanna
Moore. Most everyone was somewhere between
the Krandalls' level of casual and Hailey's, but
not Leanna. She stunned in white capris pants
and a turquoise top that matched her eyes,
chunky jewelry, and not a hair out of place. As
beautiful as the radio personality had appeared
on the billboards, the signs didn't do her justice. No wonder Renee had said they all believed
Cayden and the woman would eventually end up
together. They were absolutely fantastic standing
next to each other, as if they'd both won the best
of the best in the gene pool. Seriously, had she
come there tonight hoping to invite him to spend
time together? Why would he want to when he
had someone as dynamic as the radio deejay
vying for his attention. The woman looked at
Cayden with pure adoration.

Perhaps sensing that Hailey had arrived and was staring at him, Cayden spotted her and smiled. The curving of his lips instantly sent her pulse upward. Seeing him, Leanna glanced toward Hailey. She smiled, too, but it wasn't nearly as bright as Cayden's had been. As if to stake her claim, Leanna placed her hand on his arm, saying something to recover his attention.

"Come sit with us," the Krandalls offered, oblivious to Hailey having been put in her place by Leanna that had just occurred. "Just know that our plan in keeping you close is to have you signed up to help with the half marathon."

"I think I'm already signed up to help elsewhere. Although, to be honest, I really don't know specific details other than the event is in a couple of months." Confused, she smiled at the couple. "Venice Has Heart is a race?"

Mr. Krandall chuckled. "Venice Has Heart is much more than a race and will be here before we know it. The day starts out with the half marathon that Saturday morning," he said as they made their way toward a group in the corner. "Afterward, there are different booths, all geared to make people more heart healthy. There will be blood pressure checks, educational bits, relay races and bouncy houses for the kids, that kind of thing."

"There's a vegan cook-off competition. Some

of the vendors will be selling veggie burgers and other vegan food options to broaden dietary palates and introduce things folks may not have ever tried so they can know how tasty healthy eating can actually be," Mrs. Krandall added, waving to someone as they passed a table. "There will be relay races for the kids, face painting, that kind of thing, too. It's just a great day all the way around with something for everyone. It's one of our favorite days of the entire year and takes about a year's worth of planning."

"It sounds wonderful." She smiled at the woman. "If you're signing me up to help with the race, I assume you're in charge of it?"

"This is the third year of the Venice Has Heart event," Mrs. Krandall explained. "Bobby and I have put together the half marathon portion each year. Usually, we get to meetings early, but we picked our grandson up from band practice and ran him home this evening. He's involved in so much that his mom and dad can't always get him to and fro. We're glad to come to the rescue."

Her husband chuckled. "Listen at her acting as if we're late when we still arrived on time despite picking our Robert up from middle school."

Hailey smiled as the couple bantered back and forth all the while introducing her to the other race volunteers. Their energy was impressive, as was how welcoming they were. This, she thought. This was exactly the sort of thing she'd been hoping to become a part of. She liked these people already and they strove to do good in the world.

"Linda, you aren't trying to steal away one of my medical volunteers, are you?" Cayden hugged the woman, then shook Mr. Krandall's hand. "Hello, Bob."

The older couple beamed at him with obvious affection.

"Hailey didn't tell me that she was one of your volunteers or I *might* have left her alone." Mrs. Krandall laughed. "Probably not, but maybe."

"No?" Cayden tsked his tongue. "Sorry, Linda, but I have other plans for Dr. Easton during Venice Has Heart."

"Doctor? Good for you." Linda glanced toward Hailey, admiration on her face. "You should have told me that there was little chance he'd let me have you."

"Sorry," she apologized at the woman's playful scolding. "I honestly didn't know what all Cayden had in line for me."

"He'll have you doing more than refilling water bottles and cheering on our runners," Linda chuckled. "But he could stick you in the medical tent that morning in case any of our runners have issues. We'd love to have you with us."

"For the record, I was going to let Hailey

choose what time frame she wants to volunteer, but if she wants to come early for the half marathon, that works for me."

"I'd love to," Hailey assured them, earning smiles from the couple.

They chatted a few minutes. Then Cayden placed his hand on Hailey's back and steered her away from the others. "You came." Had he thought she wouldn't show? "I didn't know if you would change your mind or have other plans."

Had that been a dig at her possibly having gone out with Ryan or someone else? She straightened her spine to stand tall.

"We haven't known each other long." Yes, she was purposely pointing that out yet again. "But I do my best to follow through on things I say I will do. If I'm physically able to do something I've said I would do, then that's what I will be doing."

"Noted and good to know." His lips twitched, letting her know that her response had amused him. Perhaps because her hands had gone to her hips which she hadn't realized until that moment.

She ordered her tense muscles to relax. "You're in charge of the medical volunteers?"

"Darling, Cayden is in charge of the whole production. Venice Has Heart is his baby." In a waft of something that smelled absolutely fabulous, Leanna stuck out her hand. "Hi, I'm Leanna Moore."

Not surprised that the woman had soon followed Cayden, Hailey shook her hand. "I know who you are. I've seen your billboards, but they fail to do you justice." The woman beamed. "I'm Hailey Easton," she continued. "I work with Cayden at the hospital and offered to volunteer."

The woman glanced back and forth between them. "You're a nurse?"

Hailey greatly admired nurses, but that Leanna immediately assumed that must be her role irked.

"Hailey is a hospitalist at Venice General. The hospital was lucky enough to have her start a few weeks ago," Cayden supplied, then returned his gaze to Hailey. "And, really, although Leanna says I'm in charge, it's the people like her, Linda, and Bob, and so many others who put the individual pieces together who make the event such a success."

"He's much too modest." With a plump-lipped smile and her eyes conveying so much more than mere admiration, Leanna patted Cayden's cheek with familiarity. Her beautifully manicured hand lingered on the last pat prior to slowly gliding down his chin.

Was this what he'd felt when he'd said he was jealous that she'd gone to the cookout with Ryan? Hailey didn't want to feel jealousy. She'd known

Cayden less than two weeks so how could such intense green be filling her veins? She was getting too caught up in Cayden. Especially with how much she'd missed him that week. How could she miss someone she'd only known existed for such a short time? Especially when he had never been hers to begin with?

"Dr. Wilton's modesty was one of the first things I noticed about him." Hailey hadn't been sure if he'd catch her reference to the teasing comment she'd previously made to him, but his grin said he knew exactly what she'd meant. He didn't call her out on addressing him so formally and Hailey wasn't quite sure how she felt about that. Despite what he'd said, was he glad she'd kept it formal when Leanna was around to witness their conversation? Enough dwelling on Cayden's relationship with the radio beauty. It wasn't any of Hailey's business and she needed to remember that. "Nice to meet you, Leanna," she automatically told the woman from a lifetime of good manners. Then she looked at Cayden, meeting his gaze. "Point me in the direction where I can be useful or at least learn what I need to know. I want to help."

Cayden introduced her to Benny Lewis, a gem of a woman who was a retired nurse and who headed up the event's medical volunteers. Hailey got the impression that Cayden might have stuck around, but Leanna called him to where she was now with another group, saying she needed his input.

"How long are you willing to volunteer, and do you have any special interests in the day's events?" Benny asked. "Knowing that will help me know best where to place you. We want to keep our volunteers happy, so they'll be back year after year."

"This is all new to me, so no special interests other than wanting to be useful. As far as how long—" she shrugged "—how long do you need me?"

Benny chuckled. "Honey, I'll use you all day if you're willing."

Hailey glanced toward Cayden. The group he was with spoke animatedly about whatever it was they were discussing, smiling and laughing as they did so. Leanna's hand rested on his upper arm, and she leaned in to tell him something, making him laugh. Hailey's heart hiccupped.

"If it's helpful, I can be there all day." Perhaps seeing him with the radio personality would be helpful to Hailey, ingraining just how out of her league he really was despite his attention the previous week. She did want to spend time with him, but it was just as well that she didn't want a happy-ever-after as she'd only get her heart broken again. "Linda and Bob mentioned helping with the race. If there's something I can do to be useful, I'd love to assist with that."

"You want to help from start to finish? That would be amazing." Benny hugged her. "It'll be a long day. But there are several of us who do just that and think it's one of the best days of each year. I'll start you in the medical tent for the half marathon, then transition you to volunteering in the blood pressure reading area. We have nursing student volunteers taking the pressures, checking blood glucose readings, that kind of thing. Any people with abnormal results are offered a brief consult with one of the provider volunteers on what they need to do to decrease their heart disease risk."

"What a wonderful event for the community," Hailey said and meant. Education was everything in living a healthier life. She knew that firsthand. Her adoptive parents had been wonderful people, but sedentary and she'd followed in their footsteps until recently.

"It is. By the end of the day, you'll be mutually exhilarated and exhausted." Benny motioned to a table where several other volunteers were gathered. "Come on. Let me introduce you to the rest of the medical crew. At least the ones who are here tonight. We have a few who couldn't attend. And, of course, you already know Dr. Wilton. He's there from start to finish. The man is tireless when it comes to getting the word out about having a healthy heart and living your best life."

Hailey had been living her best life since meeting him. Not that he was why, she assured herself, but because she was living the life she had envisioned and was creating for herself. Cayden was just one small part of her "best life."

After the introductions, Benny ran through items she had listed out on a clipboard, making sure their team would have all the necessary equipment for the day. Apparently, they'd be set up inside a large tent. A church was supplying tables and chairs and more volunteers. Another was supplying water and heart-healthy snacks. Home health, hospice, private ambulance services, and several other health agencies would have booths and activities for attendees. During the afternoon there would be a live band and a charity auction. According to Benny they'd start closing things down around six and hopefully be done between seven and eight. As she'd asked for the half marathon medical volunteers to arrive at around six that morning, Hailey agreed that it was going to be a long day. Most of the other medical volunteers were working in half-day or shorter shifts, but Hailey looked forward to being there all day. She really did want to be involved and give back to her new community and what a great way to do so. She'd even mentioned the meeting to Jamie that morning and her new nurse friend might volunteer, as well. How cool to have a friend who wanted to spend time with her?

The meeting lasted about an hour, then ended. Hailey enjoyed getting to know the medical team and said goodbye to them. Cayden made it over to them once but had quickly been summoned back to where Leanna had wanted his opinion yet again. Apparently, the woman still needed his attention as they were deep in conversation. Hailey had caught him looking her way a few times, but he'd not made it back to speak directly to her since right after she'd arrived. Not a big deal, she assured herself. The event was what was the big deal and why she was there, why they were both there. He was busy with making sure all the last-minute details were in place.

Hailey considered going to tell him bye, but decided it would feel awkward with the others around to witness her doing so. She said a few words to Benny, then to Linda and Bob, letting them know that she had volunteered for the medical tent, and would see them early on the Saturday morning of the Venice Has Heart event which was a month away.

Glad she'd gone, excited about volunteering, and conflicted about Cayden, Hailey had made it to her car when she heard him calling to her from where he'd apparently followed her out of the building.

"Hailey, wait up."

Fingers on her door handle, she turned and saw him jogging toward her. Her heart raced as if she was the one jogging. He'd come after her. That had to mean something beyond his being grateful she was volunteering, right? "Practicing for the race?"

Catching up to where she stood next to her car, he grinned. "Something like that. Are you in a rush to go?"

Her breath caught. "Not necessarily. Why?"

"I've not eaten. Do you want to grab something with me?"

She considered saying yes. She wanted to say yes. However, she forced herself to admit the truth. "I actually ate before coming to the meeting. Sorry."

He regarded her a moment. "Can I tempt you with a drink and a sunset, then? That seems to be our thing."

She was tempted. Oh, how she was tempted. But she shook her head because as much as she wanted to go, to talk with him, her emotions were running rampant after seeing him with Leanna and just how jealous that had made her. "Not tonight, Cayden, but thanks for asking."

He nodded as if he understood, but he failed

miserably if he was trying to hide his disappointment and that boosted Hailey's courage.

She opened her car door, then paused. "If you're willing, I would take you up on the offer to go shark tooth hunting, still, though. If you aren't busy, maybe we could go this weekend?"

He regarded her a few moments, then arched his brow. "You don't have other plans?"

She knew what he was asking. She'd declined Ryan's offer to go to a concert in Tampa with others she'd met at the cookout. It had sounded like a fun outing, and yet, she'd made an excuse rather than say yes.

"I don't have plans on Saturday or Sunday morning and truly would like to go to the beach." Not that she had to have him with her to do so, but going with him would be nice and she didn't see herself shark tooth hunting without him. "Maybe I'll get lucky and find the perfect big shell for my table."

"We'd have better odds of that in Sanibel," he reminded her.

"It's okay if I don't find just what I'm looking for as I'm not in a rush. If I do find a great shell, well, that's just an added bonus to spending time with you." Heat flushed her cheeks. There. She'd been obvious in that she liked him. She might as well confess, at least to herself, that she'd turned Ryan's invitation down and purposely left her weekend open in hopes of spending time with Cayden. Which was okay, just so long as she didn't get too caught up in thinking time with Cayden was something more than just fun.

"I... Sure. I'd love to take you on your first shark tooth hunt. Does Saturday morning work? Around seven?" His eyes sparkled with the glittery gold flecks that fascinated her. Ha! Everything about Cayden fascinated her. He was a fascinating man. A fascinating man who was smiling at her in a way that had her cheeks flushing further because he made her feel pretty fascinating, too. How did he do that? When he was so fabulously gorgeous, how did he make her feel as if she were the one who was worthy of adoration? Would he have looked at her the same way if he'd met her pre-makeover? If he'd seen her prior to the hair and lash extensions, prior to the dull brown to blond, prior to the weight loss? Did it matter? She didn't even like that person she'd been. Not so much because of her outer appearance, but because of how timid she'd been on the inside, allowing John to take such advantage of her heart.

"Seven works great for me." She was used to getting up early to exercise prior to having to be at the hospital. She tended to wake early even on her off days. She smiled up at him, thinking he truly was the most handsome man she'd ever met. "I look forward to finally finding a shark tooth, and maybe getting lucky and finding a shell."

"Then I'll see you Saturday morning. Don't forget to bring your water shoes and sense of adventure."

Before she chickened out, Hailey stood on her tiptoes and kissed his cheek. "Good night, Cayden. Sweet dreams."

CHAPTER SIX

"So, I TAKE this sifter thing and I wade out into the water and just scoop up a bunch of sand and shells and whatever it picks up and I'm to hope I get a shark tooth?" Hailey eyed Cayden as if he'd lost his mind. Toes digging into the sand, her big straw hat with its tied strap beneath her chin, her baggy T-shirt and loose shorts over her bathing suit, she clutched the screened scoop. "As in, go in the water where the sharks who lost these teeth are?"

"The sharks who lost these teeth are long past," Cayden reminded her, wondering what it was about her that had him so tied up in knots, that had him thinking about her more often than not. She was beautiful, but he'd dated beautiful women in the past. It was something much more potent than physical beauty that had him so hooked. And that good-night kiss…yeah, his dreams had been sweet, all right. He'd barely thought of anything else day or night. With his work schedule not having him in the hospital Tuesday and Wednesday, and her being off Thursday and Friday, he'd missed her and considered texting her a hundred times. He should have. His reasons for not doing so had been petty. Even after her tentative smile on Monday morning, he'd let his jealousy over her going to the cookout with another man dictate that he put some distance between him and Hailey. The moment he'd spotted her with Mrs. Krandall he'd admitted to himself that he was behaving like a Neanderthal and was only depriving himself of the most fascinating woman he'd ever met. No more. "Besides," he continued. "You don't have to go out into the water that far. Just follow me, do what I do, and you'll be fine."

She eyed him skeptically, not budging from where she stood next to where he'd placed their things on the sand. He'd not unpacked their bag but would later if they decided they wanted to relax and watch the waves. He'd packed a blanket, sunscreen, the small medical kit that was always in his beach backpack, and even a small cooler with drinks and snacks in hope of extending their time together. Maybe she'd agree to lunch at one of the restaurants they'd drive past on their way back to her place.

A strong breeze whipped at them and she grasped hold of the brim of her hat, the other clasping the sifter. "What if I don't want to do what you do? What if I prefer to watch?"

"You want to just watch?" He arched a brow. "Do I need to remind you that you're the one who suggested we do this today? That you are here to find your first shark tooth? No sitting on the sidelines allowed."

She wrinkled her nose. "A woman has a right to change her mind."

He laughed at her dubious expression. "Come on, Hailey. You're going to have fun. I promise."

That's when he noticed the gleam in her eyes. "You big faker. You're already having fun."

Her lips twitched and her eyes danced with mischief. "Who says I'm having fun?"

If ever he'd heard a challenge, she'd just issued one with her flirty tone and lowered lashes.

"Me." Catching her off guard, he grabbed her at the waist, hoisted her over his shoulder, and headed toward the water.

"Cayden! Stop! What are you doing?" she demanded, laughing. "Oh, no, you're not," she warned as he waded into the water, his feet sluicing through the incoming wave. "Cayden, put me down. Seriously, you're going to hurt yourself. Put. Me. Down."

Enjoying having her in his grasp, Cayden walked farther into the water. "Don't worry. I plan to."

"Put me down on my feet while I'm not in the water," she clarified, squirming in his grasp. Her body was warm against his and she smelled good, like citrus blossoms. Probably an after-effect of her sunscreen, but he wanted to breathe in and let her permeate every part of him.

"Why would I want to do that when the view is so great from where I'm at?" he teased.

"I wouldn't know. All I can see is your backside!"

He laughed. "Poor you."

"It's not that bad, but—"

"You trying to sweet-talk me by saying you like my bum?" He definitely liked the sweet curve of hers in his periphery as he had her draped over his shoulder, the feel of her in his grasp.

"No, I'm not saying I like your bum." She wiggled as he continued farther out. "I'm saying you're going to drop me. Seriously, Cayden, put me down before you do."

Cayden took another step, using caution to make sure he had solid footing as another wave came in, hitting him just above knee level. He was far enough out now that the water would be midthigh if a bigger wave came in.

"Cayden, the water is going to knock you down."

"Then you should be still so I can keep my

balance," he warned jokingly. Surprising him, she instantly quit wiggling. "That was quick."

"I don't want to end up in the water." She was still stiff in his hold.

"Now, where's the fun in going to the beach and not getting wet?" A wave came in and water splashed onto his shorts hem.

"That's what you're supposed to be showing me, how fun looking for shark teeth is, right?" Her voice held an edge and he tried to decide if she was playing him again. "Getting tossed into the water was not part of the plan."

He gave an exaggerated sigh. "I guess you're right." He slowly slid her down his body, keeping a tight hold until her feet were firmly planted on the sand with the water rushing around their legs. To keep her hat out of the way of his chest, she had to look up and she remained doing so when she was set upright on her own two feet. Whether from the coolness of the water or how she pressed against him, goose bumps prickled her skin. His, too, but he knew exactly what had elicited his reaction. It wasn't the water. As her body had lowered, she'd wrapped her arms around his neck and if he held her this way much longer, he'd have to dunk himself prior to heading back to shore to keep from embarrassing himself. He cleared his throat. "I must be getting soft in my old age because in my younger years you'd be swimming back to shore about now."

"You're wrong." Her arms clinging tightly around his neck, almost as if she were afraid to let go, she shook her head. "I wouldn't."

"No?" Something about her tone, the way she clung to him, had him looking at her closer. The teasing light in her eyes was gone and he knew the apprehension that shone there had nothing to do with their flush bodies. His stomach knotted. "Can you swim, Hailey?"

She shivered against him. "No."

He tightened his hold at her waist. "Why didn't you say so earlier?"

Pink tinged her cheeks. "It's a bit embarrassing to not be able to swim at my age."

"Nothing to be embarrassed about, but something we should rectify." As much as he was enjoying having her pressed to him, knowing she couldn't swim, he wanted her out of the water. He scooped her back up and began carrying her back to shore. Only this time, he didn't toss her over his shoulder, but rather, held her against him where he could see her face.

"We don't need to rectify anything, and I can walk, you know," she protested, but she wasn't trying to get down and almost seemed relieved that he held her. Although, probably it was more a relief that she would soon be back on the beach.

Rather than immediately put her down when they reached the shoreline, he brought her beyond where the waves stretched to powdery dry sand, then he lowered her.

"I know and it's a lovely walk you have, too." He hoped to ease the twists in his gut. Whether the idea that he could have tossed her into the water without knowing she couldn't swim or from how her warm body had been pressed to his had caused the kinks, he wasn't sure. Probably a combination of both. "If you're going to live in Florida, you need to know how to swim."

Not that he had any say in the matter, but he wouldn't let her not learn how.

From beneath her oversized hat, she stared at him. "Is it a prerequisite or something? No one gave me that memo when I bought my house."

"No, but it should be." He appreciated her attempt at humor now that she was safely on ground, but he saw the vulnerability in her gaze, the self-disgust that she couldn't do something she thought she should. Heart squeezing at her vulnerability, he brushed his fingertip over her chin. "How is it that you never learned to swim, Hailey?"

Swallowing, she shrugged and stepped back from him. "My parents were older and weren't interested in water activities. As I reached an age where I could have learned on my own, I was busy with studying and school stuff. Learning just never came up."

"Until you decided to move to a state that is surrounded by water on three of its four sides," he pointed out, missing the warmth of her body against his. To distract himself, he bent to pull the blanket from his backpack and spread it upon the sand and tossed his sandals onto opposite corners to keep the wind from lifting them. He'd changed into his water shoes earlier but didn't want to wear them now as he didn't like the feel of wet sand in his shoes. He'd switch to his sandals prior to their leaving. He put his backpack down on the other end to hold the blanket in place.

"My moving to Florida shouldn't be a problem since I plan to stay out of the water. I can enjoy living in Florida without getting more than my feet wet. Well, except for perhaps when you're around." Her color had returned now that she was safely on the beach, but her teasing smile wasn't enough to dissuade him.

"You need to know how to swim, Hailey." He wasn't sure why her knowing seemed imperative to him. But it did. What if he'd tossed her into the waves? What if she went to the beach with someone else and didn't reveal her inability to them and they tossed her? What if something happened to her? His rib cage caved in around his chest, squeezing so tightly he couldn't breathe. Yeah, she needed to know how to swim.

"You want me to enroll in a class?" She furrowed her brows. "I'd be in there with all the little kids. No thanks. This has caused me enough humiliation for one lifetime."

Which sounded as if there was a lot more to the story.

"No need for classes with kids. I can teach you," he offered. He wanted to teach her. For lots of different reasons.

"You?" She eyed him through narrowed eyes.

"Don't sound so incredulous. I know what I'm doing. I worked as a lifeguard during high school. We offered swimming courses that I assisted in teaching."

She snorted. "Of course, you did."

"What's that supposed to mean?"

She shook her head. "Nothing."

He lifted her chin. "Tell me."

"It's just not surprising that you're an expert at swimming."

"I'm not sure I'd say I'm an expert, but I am qualified to teach you and you need to learn. The good news is that with me teaching you, you'll have private one-on-one instructions."

From where she stood on the other side of the blanket, she eyed him. The rise and fall of her chest was a little too rapid for her to be as indifferent as she pretended. "Just as you're teaching me to find shark teeth? Because so far, we're batting zero."

"The day has barely begun."

Her chin lifted, pulling free from where he touched her, but a smile played about her lips. "True, but all I'm saying is that I haven't found any teeth yet and you did promise that I'd find one."

How she went from vulnerable to using those big blue eyes to turn him inside out in a completely different way was testament to just how under her spell he was. That had nagged at him all week, but at the moment, basking in her smile, all that mattered was Hailey.

"You will, Hailey. Just as you will learn to swim."

Hailey did find a shark tooth. She found around twenty fossilized shark teeth of various sizes and breeds. Not that they'd looked them up yet, but Cayden had identified several of the teeth as makos and one as a sand tiger tooth. She'd sifted out several fossilized stingray bones and a horse tooth, too. Not that she'd have known what they were had Cayden not told her.

She'd not gone out beyond midcalf into the water. When she did so, she was fully aware that Cayden's return trips into the sea to dip out more sand and shells coincided with hers and that he always put himself out farther in what was a protective move in case she lost her footing. His automatic chivalry was sweet and something she wasn't accustomed to. John had teased her mercilessly about her inability to do something so "childish" as knowing how to swim. As she was making herself into the woman she wanted to be, she really should learn to swim.

Now they sat back on the familiar blanket that she'd become quite fond of, eating apples he'd stored in a small cooler. The cold juicy fruit was delicious.

"Thank you for bringing snacks. I wasn't expecting to be so hungry."

"Being in and around the water always works up my appetite." He gestured to the apple. "These are always a good option for a quick pick-me-up."

She nodded. "How long have you been coming out here?"

He shrugged. "All my life that I can recall. When I was a child, prior to their divorce, and separately after, my parents often rented a vacation house in Venice. It was always my favorite beach to visit."

"Because of the shark teeth?"

He grinned. "Probably. That was something different from the other places where we vacationed, and I was all boy."

He was still all boy. Well, man. In the water, his body pressed against hers had been all solid, strong man. She'd never been picked up and thrown over someone's shoulder. Cayden hadn't hesitated when doing so, making lifting her seem effortless. As apprehensive as she'd been of being in the water, deep down she'd known he wouldn't let anything happen to her and she'd been stunned at someone lifting her that way, that someone *could* lift her that way. He made her feel...dainty and feminine.

"Were you serious about teaching me to swim?"

His gaze cut to hers. "Absolutely. I want to teach you. I don't like the thought of you not knowing how to safely get yourself out of the water."

Her as in her specifically or just that he didn't like anyone not knowing how?

"Why?"

His grin was lethal as he said, "Because you never know when some man is going to toss you over his shoulder and throw you into the sea."

"You didn't throw me into the sea," she reminded him, swallowing back how being with him made her feel, with how just sitting on a blanket and eating fruit felt surreal and special.

"No, but I could have since I didn't know. Good beach advice would be to make whomever you're with aware that you don't swim."

"Now you're my beach expert, too?" At his look, she relented. "Fine. I should have told you. Like I mentioned, my parents were older and there were a lot of things I didn't do during my childhood that many would consider as standards, like learning to swim." Ecstatic to be out of the foster system, she'd been content to be in her room with a good book and her parents had never discouraged her from doing just that since they'd also been lifelong readers. She'd loved the peace, the stability they'd brought into her chaotic life, but maybe she should have stepped outside of the comfort zone they'd created for her. "In the future, I promise to make anyone I go to the beach with aware of my inability to swim."

He crunched into the last bite of his apple, put the core into a bag in his backpack, then wiped juice from his fingers. "In the future you won't need to since you're going to learn."

He sounded so confident that Hailey had no choice but to believe him. Why not? Thus far he had proved brilliant at all he did. Why should teaching her to swim be any different?

"Just when and where are these lessons going to take place?"

"My condo complex has a pool. I can teach you there or we can go—"

A scream sounded from down the beach, preventing Cayden from finishing his answer. Immediately to his feet, he took off down the beach in the direction the distressed cry had come from. Grabbing up his backpack where she'd noticed a first aid kit earlier, Hailey quickly followed.

Please don't be a shark attack, she prayed, hating that her brain immediately had gone there. *Please don't be a shark attack.*

Seeming paralyzed in the waist-deep water, a teenaged girl flailed her arms. Hailey didn't see any red discoloration the way it seemed to instantly appear in the movies when a shark attacked so maybe it was something else. But all she could think was that they were at the shark tooth capital of the world and there had to be a reason that it was the perfect environment for creating fossils like Cayden had told her.

Regardless of what it was, the other teens who'd been in the water with her seemed frozen, too, staring at their friend rather than going to where she was until finally one young man snapped out of whatever had taken over him and he began cutting through the ten or so feet that separated him from where the girl screamed in panicked agony. That Cayden reached her at about the same time the teen did said something about how fast he'd gotten there. Perhaps because of his lifeguard training, or maybe just because of his natural athleticism, the man could move.

Again, there didn't seem to be much he couldn't do and do well.

"What happened?" he called as he closed in on where the girl was still thrashing her hands as if trying to shoo something away.

Scared to go into the water and knowing she shouldn't as she might create another emergency, Hailey hesitated at the shoreline, a cold wave lapping at her ankles and sending shivers over her body. What if Cayden needed the first aid kit?

What if whatever had hurt the girl hurt him?

"Something bit me. On my leg," the girl cried between sobs. "It burns bad."

Burns. That wouldn't be a shark bite, would it?

"Careful in case whatever got her is still around," he warned the teen boy who seemed as unsure of what to do as Hailey felt from where she stood. "Sounds as if it may have been a jellyfish. Let's get her out of the water so we can figure out what's going on."

A jellyfish. That was way better than a shark in Hailey's eyes, although with the way the girl was crying, perhaps she didn't think so.

Cayden was still talking, but the waves drowned out whatever he was saying. Feeling helpless as she waited, Hailey reminded herself that for her to go into the water would be more of a hindrance than a benefit. For her to go out as far as the girl was when she couldn't swim could possibly create a second crisis, so logic said to stay put and to just be ready to help once they got the girl to shore.

Logic also said to call for emergency help. Pulling her phone from where they'd put it into his bag earlier in the day, Hailey dialed the three-digit emergency number, all the while keeping her gaze on the trio in the water. Please, please, please be okay. The girl and Cayden.

"This is Dr. Hailey Easton. I'm at Caspersen Beach. A teenaged girl is injured and is currently being assisted out of the water. Not certain as to the cause or extent of her injuries at this point."

Cayden and the young man guided the sobbing girl to the beach. Once beyond the water break, they lowered her onto the sand.

"Good. You called for help and grabbed my bag," Cayden praised, noting what Hailey held and that she was on the phone with emergency services.

Hailey had zero experience in acute emergency care of aquatic animal attack injuries. Not that she was sure that it was a jelly that had injured the woman. Her knowledge of jellyfish was limited to books and movies. Beyond her inability to swim, she felt ill prepared to deal with the current situation and she didn't like it. She'd always aimed high, to be the best she could be, not incompetent. At the moment, she felt at a huge disadvantage.

"Definitely a jellyfish injury," Hailey informed the dispatcher as she grimaced at the girl's left leg where a clearish purple tentacle wrapped around her thigh and ran down her leg. The skin beneath the detached tentacle welted a deep red as did an area on the girl's right palm, probably caused from when she'd reacted to the jelly's tentacle at her leg and tried to remove it. Wanting to help medically if needed, she handed the phone to the teen boy who'd aided Cayden getting the victim out of the water. "Here, talk to the dispatcher and keep her informed of whatever we say."

The boy looked unsure, but took the phone while Hailey knelt next to where they'd laid the girl on the sand.

Rather than immediately check her, Cayden glanced around them on the sand. Quickly spotting a shell, he got it. "This isn't going to be pleasant for you," he told the teen, "but I need to get the tentacle off you immediately. Hold still."

Hailey's Ohio hospital and emergency room rotations hadn't prepared her for jellyfish sting injury. Inadequacy hit. She wasn't working in the emergency room and by the time an admitted patient made their way to her, any acute reaction would have been handled in the emergency department. But she needed to know basics of emergency care when living near the ocean. The girl was hysterical and going into shock, possibly even beginning an allergic reaction to the venom, and that, Hailey could assist with. So, while Cayden used the shell to scrap where the tentacle clung to the girl's skin, taking care to press with enough force to remove all bits of the tentacle to stop the release of more venom into her system, Hailey placed her hand on her inner wrist for the dual purpose of checking her pulse and in hopes of distracting the teen from what Cayden was doing. They needed to calm her down as her hysteria would only exacerbate her reaction to the jellyfish's venom.

"What's your name?" she asked, making mental note of the girl's tachycardic heart rate.

"Sasha," the teen boy answered when the girl continued to sob rather than answer Hailey. Her hysterics made getting a respiration count a bit trickier, but Hailey paid close attention to her breathing pattern.

"Hi, Sasha. I'm Dr. Easton and that's Dr. Wilton. We work at Venice General," she told the girl, keeping her voice calm and hoping to reassure both her, the boy, their other friends and the small crowd that were gathering around them.

The girl's panicked gaze cut to Hailey and her

cries eased enough for her to ask, "Am I going to die?"

"No, you're not going to die," Hailey answered, even though it was possible if the girl had an intense enough reaction to the venom. Sasha was crying so profusely that it was difficult to tell if her runny nose and breathiness were from her sobs or if she was having a more intense than normal reaction to the sting. Hailey winced as blotchy red whelps that seemed to be multiplying while Hailey watched began covering Sasha's arms and legs.

"We're going to take good care of you and more help is on the way." She took the girl's uninjured hand into hers and gave it a gentle squeeze. She didn't want to alarm Sasha further but if Cayden had an antihistamine they could give her, then the sooner the better. "Cayden, Sasha has a rash. Do you have anything in your medical kit that I can give her for that?"

Apparently, he'd satisfied himself with the removal of the tentacle from her skin or decided that treating the rash took precedence. "Hand me my bag. I should have something to help."

She did so, and he pulled out the first aid kit, along with a water bottle. He handed the water bottle to a bystander.

"Pour out the water in this and fill it with sea water," he instructed as he unzipped the medical kit. "Sasha, have you ever had an allergic reaction to anything?"

"She's allergic to peanuts," the teen on the phone with the emergency dispatcher replied, answering for the girl again.

"Anything else?" Cayden asked, his gaze on the girl.

Tears streaming from her puffy eyes and down her face, Sasha shook her head, then swiped at her runny nose. She coughed and it had a wheezy sound.

"Sasha, I want you to open your mouth for me," Cayden instructed. "I need to look at your throat."

The girl did so. Cayden didn't say anything as he looked, but his gaze flicked to Hailey's for a millisecond and she knew what he'd seen, what she'd already suspected was happening.

Sasha's throat was swelling.

Why didn't it surprise her when Cayden dug into his medical kit and pulled out an epinephrine auto-injector? Was the man ever not prepared?

"You're not allergic to a medication called epinephrine?" he asked yet again, wanting to be sure the girl didn't have an allergy to the adrenaline.

"Not," the girl said, coughing again. "Just peanuts."

"She used a pen like that when she reacted to peanuts on a school trip once," the young man supplied.

"Sasha, most people don't react to jellyfish stings so intensely, but unfortunately, you are," Cayden told the girl whose brows lifted above her puffy eyes. "I'm going to give you the injection into your leg to slow, and hopefully stop, the reaction you're having to the jellyfish venom."

He didn't give the girl time to protest, just popped the injector against her injured leg in the thigh, delivering the possibly lifesaving medication in the process. When done, he tossed the device by the backpack, then took the water bottle from the bystander who'd done as he'd instructed. Cayden poured the seawater over the area the jelly fish had stung, then gently patted the area dry with a towel from his bag. Digging through his medical kit, he pulled out a tube of steroid cream and squeezed some onto the girl's leg, gently spreading a thin layer over where she'd been stung.

Hailey noticed the red line across Cayden's hand and winced. "You're stung, too."

"Got that when we were still in the water." He didn't look up from where he worked on Sasha's leg. When satisfied that the sting on her leg and hand were coated, he squirted a bit of the cream on his own hand.

In the distance, sirens blared and Hailey sighed in relief that the girl would soon be on her way to the hospital. She'd be treated in the emergency department, and the determination would be made of whether or not she needed to be admitted for overnight observation based upon how she responded to the epinephrine, any additional medications the paramedics administered, and how she did after a few hours of being watched.

Within minutes, the girl was loaded into the back of the ambulance and on her way to the hospital.

"Thank you," the teen boy told them, taking off so he could follow the ambulance to the hospital with his friend.

Clapping erupted around them. Hailey joined in, clapping for Cayden and what he'd done for the girl. His cheeks turned pink, and he tried dismissing what he'd done. "Just doing what anyone else would have done."

Hailey's heart squeezed at his humility. She didn't want to keep comparing the two men, but she couldn't help herself. John would have been calling every media outlet in the area, expecting to be heralded a hero on the nightly news. Cayden on the other hand, got a phone number from one of the teens who'd been with the girl so he could call and check on her progress.

As the bystanders dissipated, Hailey gathered

his things, putting them into the backpack and waited for him to finish talking with the girl's friends. When he had, they headed back to where they'd left their things farther down the beach.

"What just happened made me realize I need a living-near-the-sea emergency medicine crash course," she admitted as they made their way over the sandy beach.

"You'd have been fine if I hadn't been here."

She shook her head. "I wouldn't have. Beyond the fact that I couldn't have gotten her out of the water, not once have I ever treated a jellyfish sting. I mean, what other living on the Gulf of Mexico things do I need to know?"

"Other than how to swim?"

"After what just happened you may never get me to agree to go in the water again." But even as she said it, she acknowledged that she did want to learn. She'd hated knowing that if Cayden had needed her that she'd have had to stand ashore and helplessly watch, that if he hadn't been there, she wouldn't have been able to help Sasha to shore.

"What happened with Sasha is a rarity when you consider how many people get into the water. Beyond that, most who encounter jellyfish and do have the misfortune to be stung, don't have anaphylactic reactions." He held up his hand. "Like me for instance."

"True, but I don't think I'm going back in beyond where I can walk and see all around me." She winced at the red mark on his hand. "I'm sorry you got hurt. Is there anything I can do?"

"Kiss it and make it better?"

Hailey's breath caught. "If you think that would help."

He held out his hand. "Only one way to know for sure."

Swallowing, Hailey touched her lips to his hand, taking care to avoid the steroid cream by kissing just to the side of his injury.

"Better already," he assured her, smiling at her in a way that could almost convince her that her kiss truly had made him feel better. "For the record, I plan to teach you to swim in a pool, Hailey. Not in the open sea."

"I… I do want to learn." Because she didn't want to limit herself. Not ever again. "However, learning to swim isn't likely to change how I feel about getting into the ocean. But we'll see."

Because if she truly didn't want to limit herself then she had to be open to the possibility that she might change her mind.

"We'll start with learning to swim. If, after you've mastered swimming, you want to venture outside the pool, then we will. No pressure."

She didn't comment on his "we will." Who knew what the future held? For now, she was just going to appreciate that she got to spend the day with an amazing man who was kind and patient and had acted heroically with his only motivation being to help the teenager. Plus, he acted as if own injury was no big deal rather than milking it for all it was worth. Since she'd asked if there was anything she could do, she didn't count his request for her to kiss his hand and make it better. She'd been so fearful for him and the girl when they'd been in the water, she wanted to wrap her arms around his neck and kiss him for real in gratitude that he was okay, that he'd saved Sasha, both in the water and on land.

"I'm quite impressed that you had an epinephrine pen in your medical kit. I wasn't expecting that level of preparedness."

"No?" The corners of his eyes crinkled with his smile. "My sister is allergic to bees. I always keep a pen handy, just in case."

"You have a sister?" Did she sound as envious as she felt? How often had she wished for siblings?

He nodded. "Casey is older than me by a couple of years. She and her husband live in Atlanta, where my mother now lives, too, so she can be close to the grands. Dad lives in Tampa, so not too far away. During a visit a few years ago, Casey forgot her emergency medication injector and had to go to the emergency room to get treated. Since then, I keep one on hand."

"Amongst the many things I'm grateful for, I'm glad you had one today."

"Me, too." As they reached the blanket they'd abandoned in a rush, he asked, "You want to sit here a while, walk, or look for more shark teeth?"

"Ha, that's a trick question, right? We have already established that I'm not going back into the water."

"I'd be willing to scoop for you if you want to search for more shark teeth. Maybe you'll find a megalodon."

He would do that. But the truth was, she didn't want him back in the water, either. She was being a total wimp, but she preferred all of his body parts being where she could see them.

"As cool as finding a fossilized prehistoric shark tooth would be, I think I've had enough beach time for the day." Sasha's jellyfish encounter had been a great reminder of all the reasons she needed to be cautious with water activities beyond her inability to swim. "If you're not in a hurry, we could grab something to eat. My treat. Something took off with the rest of my apple. When Sasha screamed, I'd tossed it onto the blanket, and now it's gone."

He chuckled. "Some seagull or crab thought it was its lucky day."

Being with Cayden had Hailey thinking it really was *her* lucky day.

CHAPTER SEVEN

CAYDEN GRINNED AT how excited Hailey looked when she glanced up from where she was reviewing a patient's chart on the small office alcove behind the medical floor's nurses' station and saw him. She'd gone from calm professional to sparkling. Spotting him had given her joy and he liked the thought of his being able to make her happy. Over the past month, she'd certainly made him happy.

"Hello, Dr. Wilton," she greeted, sounding all businesslike as she glanced around to see if any of their coworkers were close by. There weren't. Keeping her voice to barely above a whisper, she asked, "Would you be interested in going on a double date with my friend Jamie and her boyfriend? She's my nurse friend from my yoga class. Remember that I mentioned she plans to volunteer at the Venice Has Heart event, too?"

"Hello, Dr. Easton." The bluest sea had nothing on Hailey's eyes. He wanted to dive in and lose himself. "Are you asking me on a date?"

Glancing around again, letting him know that despite their having seen each other numerous times outside of work, she preferred to keep their personal relationship just between them. Since neither of them wanted anything serious, it was honestly for the best that she preferred their co-workers not in on the time they were spending together outside the hospital. He doubted they were fooling many, though, especially Renee.

"Before you say yes," she warned, brushing a hair back behind her ear, "it's a working double date."

Intrigued, he leaned against her desk. "A working double date? You'll have to explain that one to me as I have no idea what you're talking about."

She laughed. "Probably not, but no worries. It's not anything too strenuous. I'm not putting you to doing landscaping or some other type of tough manual labor."

"I wouldn't be opposed to helping you with your landscaping or any other manual labor that you need to have done." He enjoyed the time they spent together.

"Good to know and something I'll keep in mind. But this is much better than that. It's a restaurant that my friend wants to try." She sounded so excited that he couldn't help but smile. He did that a lot around her. "You pay to learn how to cook a particular meal and do so with a chef guiding you through each step. Afterward, everyone sits down to eat the meal together. Someone Jamie works with mentioned to her how much fun they'd had when they went, and we agreed it sounded like something interesting to try." The term puppy dog eyes came to mind with how she looked at him. "Say you'll go with me."

"You know I'm not going to tell you no, right?"

Hailey grinned. "I'm hoping you're not because she's already made reservations for this Saturday night. We were afraid to wait because the only reason we got an opening on such short notice is that we were the first to reach out after they'd had a last-minute cancellation."

Saturday night. Cayden's excitement tanked. "I'm the cardiologist on call for the hospital this weekend."

Her excitement visibly fizzled.

"Sometimes I only get a few calls. Sometimes I'm there the whole weekend." He'd never really minded too much, but the disappointment on Hailey's face had him wishing he could assure her he would be able to be there the entire time for their double date. "But I usually don't make any big plans because my time isn't my own and I should be prepared for whatever the shift throws at me."

"I forgot about you being on call," she admitted, her disheartenment palpable. "I definitely understand that you have to work. Actually, that will be me having to be at the hospital next weekend for my turn on the weekend work rotation."

Which meant his seeing her would be limited to whether or not she wanted to go out after her shift ended rather than spending an entire day with her as they'd done the past two weekends.

"Just because I usually keep my schedule clear doesn't mean I can't go with you, Hailey. I just can't guarantee that I won't have to bail last minute if I get called in to the hospital." He looked directly into her big eyes, wanting to see the sparkle back in them. "I'm willing to chance it if you are."

Because he didn't want her to ask someone else to go on the double date. She hadn't mentioned the Ryan guy and Cayden hadn't asked. What had been the point when he and Hailey had been together more often than not? Either of them were free to see someone else if they chose. Neither wanted forever and eventually, they would go to just being friends.

"I'm not sure how much fun it would be to take a couples cooking class by myself if you got called away, but…" She seemed to be considering and for a moment he thought she was going to say she'd just ask someone else, and despite his previous thoughts, his breath caught as he waited for her to continue. "Let's try," she suggested, "and I'll keep my fingers crossed that you don't get called in."

Yeah, he would keep his crossed, too. She'd understand work-related things came up. The past two weeks had been fun.

"Perfect. It's a date." As he said the words, he realized what he'd said. A date. He didn't date.

"A double date," she corrected, then smiled at him so brilliantly that his heart did a funny flip-flop. Did she have any idea how much she dazzled him? He really didn't think so as most of the time she seemed to question herself. She was such a sweet contradiction, one moment exuding bold confidence and another completely blind to how great she was.

"It's been a long time since I've been on a double date," he mused from where he still leaned against the desk. Not since Cynthia. Double dating felt more serious than just going out as a couple having fun. He wouldn't back out on Hailey. He didn't really want to. But perhaps it wouldn't be a bad thing if he got called in to the hospital.

"I've got you beat." She made a soft snort sound. "For me, it's been a lifetime."

"Meaning you have never been on a double date?" That surprised him. She'd been in a long-term relationship prior to moving to Florida.

Then again, he'd already deduced that her ex was a loser who was responsible for a lot of her insecurities. Cayden would have a hard time not punching the guy if he ever had the displeasure of running into the jerk.

"That's correct." She averted her gaze, looking embarrassed and as if she regretted her admission. The vulnerability on her face had Cayden retracting his thoughts on getting called in to the hospital. Hailey deserved double dates and whatever else she wanted.

"Then I'll have to make sure this first one is a good one." Which he wouldn't be able to do if he was at the hospital. She was an amazing woman and Cayden did not want to let her down the way her ex had.

"I…uh… I'm sure it will be." Her cheeks still a little pink, she lifted her gaze to his and changed the subject. "Have you been in to see Room 208 yet? The patient was admitted for a bacterial urinary tract infection that was resistant to oral antibiotic options. He's here so he can receive intravenous medication that his culture and sensitivity test showed should resolve his infection. He doesn't have a cardiac disease history other than controlled hypertension, however, when I listened to him this morning, he threw several partial beats. The EKG I ordered only showed numerous pre-ventricular contractions so that's likely what I heard. But my gut instinct was that I should have you take a look at him so I entered the consult."

"Maybe you just wanted me to have an excuse to stop by so you could ask me out," he teased, pushing himself up from where he'd been half sitting on the edge of her desk.

Her eyes widened. "No. I didn't enter the consult for personal reasons. I wouldn't do that."

She looked so horrified that he relented rather than tease her further.

"I'm joking, Hailey. I know you wouldn't. Just as I didn't stop by here just to see you, but I admit that getting to see you is an added bonus to making my rounds these days."

She regarded him a moment, then keeping her gaze locked with his, bestowed him with the sweetest smile. "Thank you. Seeing you is an added bonus, too."

Cayden's heart threw a few wild beats, thudding against his ribcage. Reminding himself that they were at work, that someone could return to the nurses' area any moment so he shouldn't pull her to him so he could kiss her plump lips, he cleared his throat. "You want to go with me to examine 208?"

She clicked a button to close the electronic medical record program, then stood. "I'd love to, Dr. Wilton."

* * *

Later that day at Cayden's office, Dr. Pennington knocked on Cayden's office door while he was at his desk, dictating his last patient's consult note. He motioned for his coworker to come in while he finished the section he'd been working on, then paused the dictation program on his phone.

"I know it's last minute," his colleague began from where he'd sat down across from Cayden's desk, "but would you swap call weekends with me? I'm on for next weekend and Layla's parents have decided to come visit."

"You want to swap call for you to take this weekend and me to cover next weekend?" Him be off during the double date and be on call next weekend when Hailey would be working—could he be that lucky that his partner was asking to do that?

"I completely understand if you can't," the cardiologist continued. "I started not to ask because of how last-minute it was, but thought I would at least check on the off chance that you didn't have anything going on. I'd asked Rob and he already had plans so he couldn't."

Excited, Cayden leaned back in his chair. "Swapping works great for me as it's this weekend that I have something going on that I was concerned I'd get called away from."

"Seriously?" Dr. Pennington looked relieved. "That's fantastic. I owe you big, pal."

"Ditto." Cayden liked it when life worked for the better for all concerned. It seemed it rarely did, but this time he'd certainly lucked out.

That evening, he and Hailey tried a restaurant in Punta Gorda and she agreed to go to dinner with him the next evening after her shift as well, but they stayed close, choosing a seafood place that had open seating next to the water. She ordered a salmon appetizer that she insisted was some of the best fish she'd ever eaten and insisted he try. She was right.

He'd have spent every evening with her, but the following evening she had her yoga class and on Thursday evening she'd said she had other plans and hadn't elaborated. He'd offered to come by on Saturday so they could do her first swim lesson, but just as she'd done each time he'd mentioned doing so over the past few weeks, she'd put him off yet again.

He wasn't used to women putting him off when he wanted to see them. He wasn't used to caring. With Hailey, he craved every moment with her. He wasn't thrilled by that truth and assumed the excitement of being with her would soon wear off. Only, he'd never experienced the excitement he felt with being with Hailey. She made everything feel new.

On Friday evening when he arrived at her house to pick her up for their cooking date, the scent of sunshine and the sea met him. Whatever air freshener she used, he liked the clean, nonperfume fragrance. It fit the crispness of her white walls and furniture with their turquoise and sea-themed accents, including the pieces they'd picked up in Sarasota that first weekend together. The place felt homey, relaxing, and an extension of her, especially the mermaid mixed-media painting he'd gifted her. He looked at the piece and saw Hailey. It's what he'd seen from the beginning, calm amidst chaos. She did calm him. She also made his world a bit chaotic.

She confused him, had him behaving in ways he didn't understand and that were completely out of his norm. For instance, why hadn't he seduced her? He wasn't blind. She wanted him. But there was something so innocent about her sexuality that, despite knowing she'd lived with a man, he'd held himself back from taking what he wanted. Maybe he even worried that sex would change things between them in ways that would be the end.

He wasn't ready for the end. Not yet.

"These are for you." He handed her the brightly colored bouquet of assorted flowers that he'd swung into the hospital gift shop to buy when they'd caught his eye on his way out of the hospital. He'd liked the yellows and bright pinks mixed in with the daisies and other flowers. The colorful bouquet had made him think of her.

"Aw, thank you. They're beautiful." She went to the kitchen and pulled out a shell-encrusted vase they'd picked up the previous weekend at a shop they'd stopped at on their drive back from Sanibel Island. She placed the flower vase on the end table beside her driftwood lamp and the shell she'd selected from the bounty they'd found. "When I bought this and said it would be perfect for flowers, I wasn't hinting for you to buy me some."

"I didn't think you were," he assured her. "I'm glad you like them."

"I do. Tonight is going to be fun," she promised, walking to the back patio door to check to make sure she'd locked it. He imagined the enclosed area's outer door stayed locked, but he was glad she took the extra precautions even with living inside a gated community. The thought had him pausing. Had he ever considered whether or not a woman in his life locked her doors?

"If I have to cook my own meal, at least I get to do it with you." Not that he minded cooking his own meal. He'd been doing so pretty much from the time his parents divorced. Casey had helped, but Cayden had definitely surpassed his sister's cooking skills.

"You say that, but you've never cooked with me to know whether I'm more of a hindrance than a help." She grabbed her purse from the kitchen bar and turned to him, smiling big as she did so. His chest did funny things when Hailey smiled at him. Things like make up beats of its own rather than follow the usual *lub-dub* normal sinus rhythm. Her face powder didn't hide the pink tinge to her nose and cheeks.

"You got too much sun today." Which surprised him as she'd diligently protected her skin during their outings.

"Yeah, it's not too bad, fortunately, but I should have reapplied my sunscreen sooner." Moving toward her front door, she smiled at whatever ran through her mind. "I was sweating it off faster than I could have reapplied, anyway."

He'd not noticed anything different outdoors, but he'd not really been paying attention, either and she might really have worked on her landscaping. "What were you doing? Lawn work? I was serious in that I'd help you."

Not that it was any of his business, but everything about her fascinated him and he wanted to do things to make her life easier.

She'd been heading toward her front door but turned to look at him and grin. "Would you believe that I was playing pickleball?"

She sounded so proud that he did believe that's what she'd been doing.

"I didn't know you played."

"A more accurate statement would have been if I'd said that I was learning to play pickleball." She gave a self-deprecating laugh. "Unfortunately, I have the athleticism of a slug so it's slow going, but I'm enjoying learning and am already better than when I started."

She moved with such grace that he couldn't imagine her not being able to do anything she wanted, but he wasn't going to argue. What he would do is take advantage of something else they had in common. He'd been playing for years as it was something he and his buddies had enjoyed since college days.

"What you're saying is that if we play, I currently have a decent chance of winning?"

She snorted. "Oh, you're pretty much guaranteed to win. I've never been good at sports, but I'm determined to up my game since it's a popular activity at our community center. Barry says I keep getting better each time we play."

Barry. Cayden's insides withered into green mush. How could she be so nonchalant about seeing another man? He bit back an expletive.

"Barry is a neighbor, by the way. He's married and I'd guess to be in his seventies."

Had she sensed his reaction? Or maybe he'd

just thought he'd held back his frustrated curse. He and Hailey were just casually dating, not moving toward anything serious, so he shouldn't care who Barry was and he sure shouldn't feel such relief that the man was nothing more than a friendly neighbor.

That he did was concerning, but not something he wanted to delve into too closely.

To do that might be having to admit things he didn't want to admit and tonight was about making Hailey's first double date dream worthy.

Later that evening at the Be the Chef cooking venue, Hailey tossed a piece of rice at Cayden, not surprised that he deflected her playful throw. He had been the perfectly attentive date. Jamie had been wowed by him. Hailey's heart was full of pride at sharing them with each other. How blessed was she that she got to have such a fun new friend like Jamie and a great date like Cayden?

"Hey, quit wasting our dinner," he ordered, but with a mischievous gleam in his eyes that warned he was already plotting his playful revenge.

From the time they'd arrived at the venue, he'd been all smiles. Mostly he'd been that way since he'd gotten to her house other than a short moment where he'd been moody when they'd been discussing her playing pickleball. She'd guessed what had been bothering him. He didn't need to know every detail of her life, but she'd quickly enlightened him, anyway. The thought that he already knew so much, that she thought of him all the time, first and last thing each day, terrified her. Being so wrapped up in him, in spending time with him, was scary as she wondered how they'd proceed when things ended. That he was still friends with Leanna gave her hope that maybe they'd find a way to be friends, too, as she couldn't imagine her new life without him as a part of it. That was what was the scariest. How had he become such an integral part of her new life when she'd meant to never let any one man dominate her time?

"I think we have a few grains to spare," she assured him. She'd be skimping on the rice, anyway, and having more of the grilled vegetables. Amazingly, she'd dropped another five pounds over the past month. Each one had required a lot of work and discipline as she was dining out with Cayden so frequently.

"You say that as if I'm not a starving man." His words lacked conviction as he tossed a grain of rice back at her.

"Hey, the both of you quit that," Jamie warned from where she and Doug worked at the meal prep station next to Hailey and Cayden. "Act your age."

Hailey and Cayden exchanged looks, grinned, and simultaneously tossed rice grains at her friend. Snorting, Jamie rolled her eyes and started to join the fun, but their chef instructor cleared her throat, putting a stop to their shenanigans.

Not surprisingly, Cayden was an excellent slicer and dicer of their vegetables, which Hailey appreciated because he distracted her to the point that her wielding a knife while standing close enough she could feel his body heat wasn't smart. She'd never been a great cook. At least, not to hear John tell it. She'd worked long hours and still prepared their meals, but her best attempts had failed to impress him. Nothing she'd done had impressed him. She'd never had great self-confidence. After spending so much of her life with John it really was no wonder that she'd spiraled downward and believed she hadn't deserved better. Other than school and residency, he'd isolated her then consistently chipped away at her self-worth. Glancing over at the man working next to her, his gaze lifted to hers. Grinning, he winked, then went back to stirring the food mixture in the cooker, completely oblivious to how his simplest gesture set off an emotional tsunami.

Happiness bubbled. She was out on a double date with the most gorgeous, wonderful man and her new friend whom she adored and seemed to adore her back. All evening, she caught herself looking his way, shocked really by how quick his smile was, how desire *for her* shone in his eyes. Concern ebbed away her happiness.

She hadn't planned to date anytime soon after her move but meeting him had changed that. When things ended, how could any man ever measure up? She was spending more and more of her spare time with him. If she wasn't careful her new life was going to revolve completely around Cayden. That terrified her. She and Cayden weren't forever. Even if she wanted them to be, which she didn't, she wouldn't be able to maintain her shiny new facade indefinitely, and eventually her new life would collide with her old and he'd see the real her, the version that never would have caught his attention.

Fake it until you make it, right? With her hair and lash extensions, facial treatments, and so forth, she had the faking it down pat.

Or maybe not as she dreamed of kissing Cayden, of doing much more than kissing him but, other than quick pecks and lots of hand-holding, she had pulled away each time. Some things couldn't be faked. What if Cayden found her as lacking as John had? What if their becoming physically involved was the catalyst to revealing what no amount of makeup and self-help books could hide?

Yeah, she was getting way too attached to Cayden, was way too caught up in what he thought of her, and as lovely as their evening was, she needed to take control of her new life back and quit planning everything around him.

CHAPTER EIGHT

"GIRL, YOU'RE NOT looking so good."

Hailey hadn't needed Renee's assessment to know that. She'd gone to bed not feeling well and had awakened feeling worse. Still, she'd headed to the hospital. She'd only been on the job a couple of months. She wouldn't miss work unless she was literally unable to move. She was moving. Barely. So, she'd work and stay masked to keep from spreading germs to her patients and coworkers. "I'll be okay."

Maybe.

Cayden didn't have any direct admissions and wasn't on call so Hailey didn't see him that morning. Just as well as she didn't want him to see her so subpar. Makeup couldn't hide her putrid color. By lunch, she gave in to Renee's demand that she reach out to the hospital administrator to see if someone could cover the remainder of her shift. Not once during med school or residency had Hailey missed a single day, but she was miserable.

Fortunately, the hospitalist coming in for the evening shift was available, allowing Hailey to head home and to bed. By evening, she admitted defeat and called out for the following morning.

She slept, woke several times, forced fluids, then fell back into fitful sleep. About dawn, she settled into a decent rest and didn't wake until almost noon. Unfortunately, she was still running a temperature and had body aches that rivaled being hit repeatedly by a baseball bat.

"Got. To. Drink." With the fever on top of her stomach issues, she was going to get dehydrated. She shuffled to the kitchen, opened her cabinets and saw nothing appetizing, then went to stand in front of her refrigerator. Nothing there appealed, either.

She got a glass of water, then headed onto the patio. Maybe just sitting there where she could see the sunshine and the lake would help. Maybe it did as she couldn't say she felt any worse. No better, but not worse. Feeling worse might be impossible, though.

"Quit feeling sorry for yourself."

Eventually, she went back to bed. She didn't recall falling asleep, but she must have as her phone ringing startled her awake. She reached for it and realized she'd missed several calls and texts from Cayden.

"You left work early yesterday and haven't responded to any of my texts. If you hadn't answered this call I was headed your way and not leaving until I put eyes on you," he told her. "Are you feeling better?"

She shook her head, grimacing as pain stabbed through her head.

"Hailey?"

Her lips stuck together as she tried talking. "Not better."

"You sound terrible."

"Thanks," she managed, opening and closing her dry mouth.

"Do you need anything?"

"To feel better. Going to sleep now." Except she needed to drink something with electrolytes, first.

After disconnecting the call, she opened a delivery app and placed an order. Drinks, crackers, soup. She had this sick thing down.

For fear she'd dose off and not wake up when her supplies arrived, she made her way into her living room, blanket, pillow, and all, and crashed onto her sofa.

Picking up the grocery bags and a package of sport drinks from Hailey's front porch, Cayden rang her doorbell again. After a minute or so, her deadbolt clicked, and the door opened.

She blinked, her long lashes sweeping across

her cheeks. Dark circles and makeup rimmed her eyes. Her hair was disheveled. She wore an Ohio State sweatshirt and a pair of loose pajama pants and had a blanket wrapped around her shoulders.

"You look terrible." The moment the words escaped his mouth he longed to take them back because he'd swear her already pale skin blanched a few more shades.

"Sound terrible." She coughed, emphasizing her point. "Look terrible. Feel terrible." Her puffy eyes met his. "What are you doing here?"

He held out her groceries as if that somehow explained why he was there. "I came to check on you."

"I'm fine."

She didn't look fine. If it was flu season, he'd think she had the flu. "Is it okay if I carry these to the kitchen?"

She moved aside. "Enter at risk of catching whatever I have."

"I'll take my chances." He generally didn't get ill, but he'd use caution, making sure not to touch his face and would wash his hands well.

"Okay." She looked lost for a moment, then appeared overcome with exhaustion. "I need to go to bed." With that, she turned, stumbled, and righted herself just as he reached her, groceries still in tow. "Just need sleep."

"Have you eaten today, Hailey?" He placed

the groceries on the floor to free his hands and followed her, not touching but close enough he could catch her if she started going down.

She paused in her slow shuffle. "No."

"Once you're in bad, I'm going to cook you something." He wasn't leaving her side until she was safely in bed. Like the rest of her home, the room was done up in whites and turquoise. Throwing off the color theme was a shelf loaded down with books. She'd been telling the truth about self-help books. There were dozens of them. The thing he liked most was a painting of a young girl staring off into the blurred distance. Had she gone to one of the markets without mentioning it to him?

"I bought soup." He had to strain to hear her mumbled words.

"I'll get one of the sport drinks. You could use the electrolytes. Then, I'll heat the soup."

She didn't argue, just crawled into her bed and pulled the covers over her body. Eyes closed, she grunted something that sounded like thanks.

With one last worried glance, he left her room, grabbed the groceries, and proceeded to her kitchen. He should have come over when he hadn't heard back from her the previous night. He'd tried texting and calling but had just thought she'd gone to bed early. When she still wasn't responding by this evening, he'd had to know she was okay. She wasn't okay.

He found a metal straw, poured some of the sport drink into a cup, then brought it to her room.

"Hailey, let me help you sit up long enough for you to sip on your drink."

She roused, raising a little, and taking the smallest drink in history prior to her head returning to her pillow. He placed the cup on a painted mermaid coaster on her nightstand, then headed back to her kitchen.

He unpacked her groceries, putting them away, with the exception of the soup and saltine crackers. He heated up the chicken noodles, spooned out a small bowl, put a few crackers on her plate, then headed to her room. She'd gone back to sleep. Did he wake her or let her sleep? If not for the fact that she'd not eaten or drunk much, if anything, all day, he'd let her rest. But if he couldn't get liquids inside her orally, she would need an intravenous infusion.

"Hailey, wake up. You need to eat."

She mumbled.

"Hailey." He shook her shoulder. "It's time to eat and drink. If you can sit up, I'll feed you."

Her eyes opened and she peered at him. "Why are you in my bedroom?"

"Not for the many reasons I'd like to be. Actually, that's not true. With you ill, this is right where I want to be, taking care of you." His words stunned him, but he assured himself that's what friends did for each other. "Let's get you scooted into an upright position."

"May not stay down. Or in." She winced. "Not been a good twenty-four hours."

"Noted. You still need to eat and drink. If you can't keep anything in, you're going to Venice General for intravenous fluids."

"I—thank you." She attempted to push herself off the pillow but failed. Cayden helped her to sit with her back against her headboard.

"Take a drink." He held the cup for her while she sipped through the straw. "Can you feed yourself or do you need help?"

"I'll try." She took a few bites then seemed bored with her food.

"Try or I'm bringing you to the emergency department to get fluids." Seeing her so weak was wrecking him and he needed to be doing something, anything, to make her feel better.

"No ER." Grimacing, she took another drink, then let him feed her half of the soup, watching him with hooded eyes with each delivered bite. She held up her hand. "No more. Need to sleep."

"Okay, sleep. I'll wake you for more fluids after we see if you're going to keep this down."

He wasn't going anywhere until she was improved. A lot improved.

Hailey woke with a start, having heard a noise in her bedroom. There, in the low light streaking in through her windows, Cayden stretched out in the oversized reading chair. He'd pulled it next to the bed and didn't look nearly as comfy as she felt when curled up there.

Why was Cayden in her bedroom? Why was his hand holding her forearm as if he was afraid to let go? Then the former night's events came rushing back. Cayden had come to her rescue. She had vague memories of his waking her throughout the night to drink.

She glanced at the clock, then pulled free from Cayden's touch. Oh, no. She should be at work. She was new and had no-showed. Would they fi—?

"I called last night," Cayden interrupted her panic, "and let the hospital know you wouldn't be in today."

Part of her wanted to protest at his high-handedness, but gratitude filled her. How had he known to? Not that he wasn't aware of her work schedule, just that she was surprised he'd thought to call in for her. "Thank you."

"You may not be thanking me if word gets out that I called in sick for you. That might be difficult to explain to Renee."

Hailey rubbed her temple. Yeah, Renee getting wind wouldn't be good.

"How are you feeling this morning?"

"Alive," she mumbled. "Alive seems an improvement from yesterday."

"You were pretty rough when I got here."

She reached for the drink he had by her bed, took a sip, then nodded. "I'm embarrassed that you saw me like that." Grimacing, she touched her hair, then covered her face with her hands. "And like this."

"You're beautiful, Hailey. No makeup required."

Mortified that he'd seen her without makeup— no, that wasn't right. He was seeing her with two-day-old makeup she'd slept in. She probably looked like a clown. "You've obviously caught whatever I have. Delirium is setting in."

Looking much too serious, he shook his head. "No delirium, just good taste. Are you hungry?"

She nodded.

"Do you feel up for toast? When I was putting away your groceries, I noticed you had purchased bread and oatmeal, too. I'll gladly make you whatever sounds good."

Embarrassed that she was just lying there while he was offering to prepare food, she scooted up, meaning to rise, but dizziness hit.

"I can make it," she said anyway, hoping the room stopped spinning so she could stand.

"I'd rather you let me."

She pressed her fingers to her throbbing temples,

thinking maybe it was her head spinning rather than the room. "Don't you have to be at work?"

"My office manager rescheduled my appointments."

Guilt hit. He was a busy man and had things to do other than nurse her back to health. He had stayed with her all night, had awakened her to drink, had helped her to the bathroom and held a washcloth to her forehead when she'd gotten ill.

"I don't want your appointments canceled because of me." She'd inconvenienced him enough.

"Already done, Hailey. I'm not going anywhere today other than staying right here so I can take care of you."

"I—okay. I'm going to go to the bathroom. Toast and a drink sound wonderful."

Having someone to take care of her was wonderful. She'd gotten sick when she'd been twelve. Her mother had held her most of the night. That had been the only night someone had held her while she was ill. Her mother, and now, Cayden.

Gratitude filled her. He truly was a kind man. And, hopefully that really was just gratitude she was feeling and not anything more because falling for Cayden would be all too easy. She couldn't do that.

Not if she didn't want to end up with a broken heart that no amount of nursing back to health would heal.

* * *

The following Saturday, Cayden eyed the sunscreen-coated woman from where she sat on the edge of the swimming pool. She swirled her toes in the pool water. Her nails were flamingo pink and her big toes each had a tiny palm tree with sparkly leaves. He wasn't a feet man, but Hailey's never failed to catch his attention. Probably because they were attached to her toned legs that were glistening in the sunlight.

"This is probably a waste of time as I've no plans to swim."

"Spending time with you is never a waste." He liked being with her. "Besides, we're focusing on floating, not swimming,"

"Show me how floating is done again." She obviously stalled, making him question again if something had happened to make her so leery of learning. She wore the same black one-piece bathing suit with a pair of shorts that she'd worn to shark tooth hunt.

He moved closer to where she sat, placing his hands to either side of her hips on the pool edge. He looked directly into her eyes. "Are you afraid of the water, Hailey?"

She moistened her lips, then took a deep breath. "Yes."

"You're afraid because you can't swim? Be assured that we're going to change that. It may take us a few days or a few weeks, but you will learn to swim."

She eyed him, then stalled further by saying, "Maybe I'm afraid because there are living things in the water that can hurt me."

"There are living things outside the water that can hurt you," he reminded her, not buying her excuse, especially as the pool water was crystal clear. "You obviously function just fine."

She feigned shock. "You're right. There are. I should go inside and cover myself in bubble wrap."

"Bubble wrap would make for an interesting swim lesson and might help you float."

Sighing, she ran her fingers along where she'd braided her hair. "You think I'm being silly, don't you?"

Silly wasn't one of the adjectives he'd use to describe her. Beautiful, brilliant, mesmerizing, frustrating, but not silly.

"What I think is that you aren't going to get past your water hang-ups until you are confident in your ability to swim. I'm sorry about what happened with Sasha, but that isn't something that happens often, Hailey. Nor does learning to swim mean that you have to go into the open sea if that's not your thing. Prior to what happened with Sasha, you wanted to learn."

"I do. It's embarrassing that I can't. It's just

that…" She hesitated. "I tried to learn once before. It didn't go well."

"You didn't have me for a teacher." He'd taught numerous kids over the years he'd worked as a lifeguard. Teaching Hailey would be his pleasure.

"Maybe I'm not someone who is meant to swim."

Eyeing her, seeing the holes in her self-confidence, he yet again wanted to hurt her ex. "Work with me, Hailey. We will get you there."

She still looked hesitant. "I don't want to upset you if I'm not able to do the things you want me to do."

"I'd never be upset with you for not being able to do something, Hailey." Surely, they had spent enough time together that she realized that. "I'd be disappointed if you didn't try at all, but never upset that you tried and failed. It's the trying part that I count as the most important."

She stared into his eyes, her gaze holding fast as his hands went to her waist. Seeming to know what he wanted, she nodded and slid forward as he guided her into the water and against him. The water only came to his waist but, with their height difference, came in just beneath her breasts. Cayden gulped.

"See, this isn't so bad." Holding her felt good, just as it had when he'd lowered her into the water at the beach. Hailey against him felt right.

"Only because you're holding me," she pointed out with a self-deprecating smile. "If you hold me like this the entire time, I'll be fine."

Cayden wouldn't mind holding her the entire time. However, he wanted to help her overcome her fears and he especially wanted her able to safely navigate in water. "I won't let anything happen to you, Hailey."

He meant in the pool, and yet, with her in his arms, how protective he felt of her gave him pause. He wouldn't let anything happen to her. Anywhere. Not if he had any say in the matter.

Clinging to him, she seemed to sense that his mind had gone deeper than the surface of what he'd said. She squeezed where she held on to his arms. "Then, let's get this over with."

"Such an enthusiastic student," he teased.

"It's not that I'm not grateful that you're spending your Saturday trying to teach me. I am appreciative. It's just that," she hesitated, seeming to not know how to express her concerns as she shrugged.

Unable to resist, Cayden leaned in to kiss her temple. Once again, her citrusy scent assaulted his senses, making him deeply inhale. But it was how the feel of his lips pressed to her, how zings of awareness shot through him that had his legs threatening to buckle. He cleared his throat. "We'll stay where you can stand up at any time you feel you need to. Just relax and trust me to keep you safe."

Too bad he didn't trust his ability to keep himself safe from how his emotions were getting so tangled up with Hailey.

"I do trust you." Seeming surprised by her admission, she stared at him with eyes so blue they shamed the pool's bright color. After a moment, she tentatively smiled and loosened her death grip on his arms. "Tell me what to do."

Cayden told her, and as she attempted to do as he asked, he kept his hands at her midsection, keeping her afloat. "We're going to keep practicing this, Hailey. We'll go from one side of the pool to the other for as many times as needed."

"As many times as needed? I hope you have all day."

"I do." His hand beneath her abdomen, Cayden guided her through the water. They made the trip several times. "You did great," he praised, helping her to her feet.

"I didn't do anything except lie there."

"That's what floating is all about. Just lying on the water."

"Without sinking," she added.

"Not sinking is an important component of successful floating." Just as keeping his gaze locked with hers was an important component of keeping his mind off how her wet suit clung to her body.

"Maybe I'll eventually float without you having to hold me."

He had mixed feelings about that. As much as he wanted her success, he liked the excuse to touch her. "Practice makes perfect."

"It'll take a lot to convince me that you weren't born perfect."

Her comment surprised him. "You think I'm perfect?"

"As close as I've encountered." Sunshine reflected off the water and her eyes, creating a surreal, almost mystical look.

"I'm far from perfect, but you make me wish I was."

She blinked. "Me?"

"It's no secret that I'm attracted to you, Hailey."

She hesitated, then, a small smile on her full lips, she placed her hands against his chest. "I'm attracted to you, too, Cayden." Her hands trembled. "How about we finish and get dried off?"

Cayden didn't need water to float. She was enough to have him soaring.

CHAPTER NINE

STARING AT HER reflection in her bathroom mirror, Hailey rubbed her plumped lips together, evenly spreading the shiny gloss. After they'd gotten back to her place, she'd showered to wash off the pool's chlorine, donned a sundress and sandals, and carefully reapplied her makeup. She'd applied lotion, styled her hair, and changed outfits twice. Butterflies danced in her belly as she stared back at her image, barely recognizing herself as the same woman she'd been just a few months ago. What would Cayden have thought of that woman? Would he have noticed her with her dull hair and her ineptitude with anything to do with beauty? Would he have looked at her the way he had while they'd been in the pool? Like he'd wanted to kiss her? To do much more than kiss her?

Hailey gulped. No doubt he had finished in her guest bathroom long ago and was waiting for her. She could hear where he'd turned on the television in the living area.

With one last look in the mirror, she left the re-
prieve of her bedroom's ensuite bath. Only, when
she went into her living room, Cayden wasn't
there. For a moment, she thought he'd tired of
waiting and had left. The shade to the glass patio
doorway was pulled back. He must be on the
covered patio.

She was quite proud of the comfy outdoor
area she'd created. She'd spent many an hour
out there already and it was one of her favorite things about the house. That and looking out
at the little man-made lake and watching birds
come and go. Fortunately, she'd not seen any alli-
gators, but was told that one occasionally sunned
along the banks. She was no more a fan of alliga-
tors than she was of sharks or jellyfish so if she
never spotted one, she'd be just fine.

His back to her, Cayden was sitting on the
comfy oversized lounger with his feet propped
up. Going around to join him, she realized he'd
fallen asleep. How cliché that she'd taken so long
getting ready that he'd dosed off? The irony of
it had her smiling.

With the freedom granted by his closed eyes,
she studied him, taking in each of his features.
His dark hair was still lightly damp from his
shower. His thick lashes spread out long over his
cheekbones. His chest rose and fell rhythmically
with each breath. He was so handsome that he

made her question why he was really there, with her, saying things like that he was attracted to her. Had her drastic makeover really been that successful? That the new her could attract someone so wonderful?

He looked so peaceful that rather than wake him, she sat down beside him, snuggling close enough that she leaned against him and closed her own eyes. She wasn't one for naps and couldn't imagine falling asleep when she was near someone as dynamic as Cayden, but being next to him, letting herself relax against him, was nice.

Only, it didn't take long for his breathing pattern to change, hinting that if he'd been asleep, he no longer was. She shifted to glance at him and met his half-lidded hazel gaze. Had any man's eyes ever been more beautiful? More mesmerizing?

He didn't say anything, just brushed his fingers along her face, skimming her hairline, then gliding along her chin ever so gently. Goose bumps prickled her skin. Her heart quivered. All of her did. His touch was reverent, as if he couldn't believe he was there *with her*. Surreal. Maybe she had fallen asleep and was dreaming.

"Cold?" he asked.

Hailey shook her head. She wasn't cold. Quite the opposite. Her insides burned. Her gaze lowered to his mouth and temptation hit so strong that she longed to know what it would feel like to kiss him for real and not the light touches they'd been playing around with for weeks. Breathing was more and more difficult. Maybe that was why she scooted so close that his breath became hers.

He didn't move, just waited to see what she was going to do. Hailey wanted to know her next move, too. She was no seductress, no siren to lure men. Yet she'd have to be blind not to see that, for the moment, Cayden was under her spell, and his breathing was as ragged as her own at just her lightest touch. His reaction had her heart racing and her body aching, and made her crave him enough that resisting temptation was impossible.

She stretched the tiniest amount, pressing her lips to his tentatively with her eyes wide open. She didn't need to watch him, though. She could feel his response, could hear the low half growl, half moan that escaped him when she lingered, tasting his mouth.

"Hailey." The way he said her name emboldened her. She placed her palms against his cheeks, marveling that she touched him, that she threaded her fingers into his hair, then pulled him to her.

"Hmm?" she whispered against his mouth,

so close she could feel the warmth of his breath. "Tell me what you want."

"You know what I want." His hands were on her now, her shoulders, her back, her bottom as he lifted her to lie upon him and molded her firmly against him to show her just how much he wanted her.

She'd never quite envisioned this moment when she'd bought the lounger, but she'd never be able to see it again without thinking of Cayden beneath her, his hands cupping her bottom as they kissed. Oh, how they kissed.

Hailey wasn't sure how long they kissed. An eternity could have passed, and it wouldn't have been enough to fully savor him. She wasn't sure how much time passed prior to her fingers sliding beneath his T-shirt, removing his T-shirt so she could run her hands over his chest and shoulders. She loved touching him, experiencing his responses. Soon, she couldn't think about his responses for her own, though. All she could do was feel.

"You're sure?" he asked.

Hailey wasn't sure of anything except that he best not stop the magic he was wielding over her body. She wasn't sure what words came out of her mouth, but they must have been the right ones because his smile was so beautifully perfect as he caressed her face.

"Hailey," he said, kissing her and forever changing her, winding her so tightly that she had no choice but to explode into tiny bits of colored confetti that floated back to earth from some heavenly place.

If there was really such a thing as grinning from ear to ear, Cayden imagined he was doing exactly that as he marveled at the woman he held close to his sweat-slickened body. Marveled because she was marvelous. As his coworker, his friend, and his lover.

His lover. Because he loved her? Right after the most amazing physical experience of his life was not the time to be contemplating his feelings for Hailey. Delirium had obviously set in, because when he looked at her he couldn't help but think that he wanted to hang on to this feeling forever.

Forever was a life sentence he'd not planned to endure.

So why did forever feel like it wouldn't be nearly long enough if Hailey was by his side?

"Anyone ever tell you that you're an amazing kisser, Hailey? An amazing everything."

"No. But then, until today, I'd only ever kissed one man."

Cayden's eyes widened. "You're kidding?"

Taking a deep breath, Hailey rolled so that she

was lying next to him rather than on him. "I wish I was," she half mumbled, not looking at him. "John was my first and only boyfriend prior to, well, um, you."

"You'd never kissed anyone other than your first boyfriend?" He'd known she wasn't overly experienced. Had liked that, even. That innocent air about her had been one of the reasons he'd not rushed their physical relationship. Had he known the intensity of what they just shared, nothing would have held him back short of Hailey herself.

She shook her head.

"How is it that you've only kissed one man other than me?"

"Men weren't exactly beating down my door."

He scooted to partially sit up and stared at her in such shock that, had her skin not still been flushed from what they'd done, she'd have blushed. "Were the men in Ohio idiots?"

She snorted. "I've mentioned that I made a lot of life changes beginning just prior to and continuing after moving to Florida." She reached up and touched her hair. "My appearance was one of those major changes. New hair, new eyelashes—" she batted them "—corrective eye surgery to lose my glasses, eyebrows, extreme diet and exercise, facials, fillers, and makeup consults with how-to classes, manicures, pedicures, the list goes on." She grimaced, then reached for her shirt. "Honestly, it's exhausting and things I'd never bothered with before. I wouldn't have had time even if I'd wanted to, not with med school and residency and John. Trying to improve one's looks is time-consuming and expensive. I started in Ohio, and my first week here I was at appointments every day, some days two or three. Now I spend my Thursdays and some Fridays doing maintenance appointments."

"You don't need to improve your looks, Hailey. You're gorgeous."

"You didn't see me before," she reminded him, putting her shirt back on.

"Doesn't matter. I'd have still found you attractive." His attraction to her went way beyond her hair and nails.

Hailey laughed a hollow sound that held more pain than humor. "You say that, but that's because you're looking at the new me. The me that, short of going under the reconstructive knife, has maximized her looks. No one found me attractive. Just John and he—" She stopped. Her gaze lifted to his, seeming horrified at what she'd just told him.

Idiots, he thought. John and every man who'd ever made her see herself in any way other than beautiful.

"He what?" Cayden prompted from where he sat next to her on the lounger.

Not looking at him despite his willing her to, she shrugged. "I prefer to think he liked me in the beginning, but honestly, he may never have. I was his meal ticket and security blanket. To put it bluntly, I was basically his sugar mama."

Her confession shocked him. Little things she'd said and done that he'd put down to feminine independence now took on a new slant. He furrowed his brows. "As a resident?"

"My parents weren't wealthy, by any means, but they had done all right for themselves. I inherited a decent chunk when their house was auctioned off as it was on a nice piece of land in a popular area in Cincinnati. Fortunately, Dad had set up a trust with his life insurance policy and the trustee rolled most of the estate sale into that investment account that I couldn't access until recently. I got a monthly living expense payment from the trust but I couldn't access the bulk of it until finishing graduate school or my thirtieth birthday—whichever came first. Thank goodness he did that as otherwise, I'm not sure I'd have anything left because John spent every penny he could get his hands on."

Whatever amount her inheritance was, Hailey was the real treasure.

"I'm on record as saying the man was an

idiot." How could the man have been in a long-term relationship with Hailey, have had her vying for his love, and been more interested in things?

"It could be argued that I'm the one who was foolish, because it was me who let him take advantage of me for so long."

"You obviously cared about him."

She nodded. "I thought I loved him and vice versa. Now, whether from time away from him or my therapy, I recognize that I was so desperate for love and attention that I was easy prey for him to swoop in and convince me that he was all I deserved."

"You deserve good things, Hailey." Everyone did. Cayden hugged her, not liking how she remained stiff in his embrace. "The best things."

"So my therapist keeps reminding me." Not seeming comfortable with his holding her, she reached for her underwear and sundress, putting them on prior to continuing. Once dressed, she walked over to stare out at the man-made lake that bordered her backyard. "I didn't date in high school. Not a single date. It wasn't because I didn't want to, but that no one asked."

The pain and embarrassment in her voice had Cayden's insides aching for her. That she'd felt the need to move away from him after what they'd just shared had his insides aching, too.

Surely, she knew there was no reason to feel embarrassment with him?

"Apparently, you've been surrounded by idiots your whole life."

She turned, met his gaze with her sad blue eyes that ripped at his heart when they'd been so happy, so full of desire, just minutes before. "I was an introvert and wasn't involved in much during my school years. At first due to bouncing from one foster home to another, but then, after my parents adopted me, because I was happy to have a family and wanted to be with them. I met John early in my college freshman year around the time my mother died from breast cancer. My father died less than a year later from a broken heart. John was the only person in my life."

"I'm sorry, Hailey." He wanted to hold her, to wrap his arms around her until she felt so loved that loneliness could never take hold again, but when he stood to go to her, she shook her head. Sensing she needed to say whatever was in her heart, he grabbed his clothes and got dressed while she continued.

"Even after I acknowledged that our relationship was over, I went with the status quo rather than making the break." She took a deep breath. "Ending things meant being completely alone in the world. That scared me."

"You've obviously overcome that fear." At her

look of doubt, he pointed out. "You moved to a state where you didn't know anyone. That takes guts."

Her expression remained dubious. "Or a really strong desire to start over where no one knew the old, boring me."

"You were never boring, Hailey." Unable to stay away a moment longer, he crossed the patio to where she stood and placed his fingertip against her temple. "What's up here is completely fascinating."

"I'm glad you think so." A tear slid down her cheek, gutting him.

"Don't you?"

She swiped at the tear, waving him off and taking a few steps away from him. "I'm working on that, too."

"As part of this big makeover you've done?"

She nodded. "I'm creating the life I want."

His brow lifted. "That sounds like a line from a self-help book."

"That's quite possible. There's a bunch of them on the shelf in my bedroom and I've read them all at least once." Glancing toward him, she didn't quite meet his eyes. "Now you realize I'm a messy work in progress and we shouldn't have done what we did a few minutes ago, not with the baggage I carry."

"Who doesn't have baggage, Hailey?"

Hailey's gaze lifted to his. "You."

He harrumphed. "You think I don't have baggage? I must put on a good show, then, because I've enough to fill an airport. We could start with the girlfriend I dated through high school and my first two years of college. I planned to marry her the summer prior to starting med school."

"What happened?"

"She got pregnant by some random guy she met on a girls' trip to Miami. I might have forgiven her, except apparently it wasn't the first time she'd cheated."

"I'm sorry."

"It gets better," he admitted, wondering how such an amazing day had turned into a confessional. "Hurt, I jumped into another relationship, which started off great. I was planning to propose, but that time it was my roommate who Cynthia cheated with. After that, I quit believing in love as I realized that when it came to women, I prefer being friends with benefits, like my relationship with Leanna was, rather than anything with promises of fidelity and forever."

Which had him circling back to his earlier thoughts about Hailey. Because no matter how much bringing up the past might make him want to recant those earlier thoughts, he couldn't. Hailey was unlike anyone he'd ever met. Beautiful in ways the eyes couldn't see, in addition to wowing him with her eyes and infectious smile. Smart, funny, trustworthy.

Fidelity and forever not only didn't feel impossible with Hailey, but rather, his heart's inevitable destiny.

Stunned by the women who had been in Cayden's life, Hailey stared at him, thinking she could toss his own words back at him. His exes had been idiots. How could any woman have had his love, have had him wanting to spend his life with her, and her to have treated his heart so callously?

Hailey just couldn't fathom it.

She also couldn't fathom how she was going to move past what they'd done earlier. They'd had sex. Good sex. Phenomenal sex. Sex that had blown her away. Sex that he'd enjoyed, too. He had been right there with her every touch and moan along the way. Not because she'd been worriedly trying to make sure he liked what they were doing. She'd been so caught up in what he was doing to her body that she hadn't been thinking, just feeling and touching and basking in such unexpected pleasure. He'd given that to her so selflessly, had made her feel so good.

Just looking at him, she wanted to grab hold and never let go. Which was foolish and why he'd just reminded her that he preferred being friends with benefits and didn't do commitment.

No doubt he wanted to make sure that, in her inexperience, she didn't mistake what they'd done to mean anything more than what it had been. Sex.

Her heart squeezed in protest. What was wrong with her that despite all her big plans and goals she'd fallen for the first guy she'd become involved with? She'd not even planned to date, had known she needed to focus on herself and not a relationship. He'd been so deliciously tempting that she'd been unable to resist, had convinced herself that she was just dipping her toes into the dating world by spending time with him. Ha. How foolish was she? Would she never learn?

"I—you're right." She stood a little straighter, needing all her strength to do what needed to be done. Self-preservation demanded she take control of her life and fortify the miniscule barriers he'd blown through to reach her vulnerable heart in such a short time. No way could she recover from a heartbreak at Cayden's hands. Her heart was much too fragile from where she'd pieced it back together after John's crushing it. No way would she go back to the weak, clingy woman she'd been, begging for John's love and attention. "I'm glad we can discuss this like adults and that we're in agreement. Promises of forever and fidelity would ruin our friendship." She didn't want to hear fake promises. She wanted... no, she did not want that. She couldn't want that. To want that would bleed her heart dry. "I owe you the biggest thank-you for what happened between us, because sex was never like that with John. Now I'm curious as to what all I've been missing out on and look forward to fully jumping into the dating world."

That she'd shocked him was obvious. His eyes had widened, then narrowed. "You plan to jump into the dating world?"

She nodded. "I haven't learned all the things I should have learned by this point in my life. Thank you for helping me realize how fun sex can be when it isn't bogged down by emotional entanglements. Is it always that good? I mean, with other people?" Realizing he could take what she'd said as her fishing for a compliment, she quickly added, "Oh, never mind. I'll find out for myself."

Nausea gripped her stomach at the thought of anyone touching her other than Cayden, but she kept her tone and expression light.

Cayden continued to stare at her in disbelief. Had his previous involvements been clingy afterward? She wouldn't cling. She knew doing so would be futile. Just look at how long she'd clung to John. She'd never do that again.

But if she continued seeing Cayden, would she

remain as determined? Or would she fall into a lifetime of desperately wanting to be loved and end up devastated?

Look at how passionate she was about him after just a few months. She had to put herself first, to preserve her new life, and not let anything or anyone steal that from her. Not even herself.

"But I think what happened between us shouldn't happen again. With us being coworkers, continuing the benefits part of our friendship would be too complicated."

"You don't want to see me again?"

Only during every waking moment.

She hated herself for the thought, for her weakness, her foolishness.

"Not outside of work and Venice Has Heart."

He raked his fingers through his hair, paced across the patio, then turned to her. "Did I miss something, Hailey? Something I did wrong?"

She shook her head. He'd done everything right and that was the problem. "It's best if we don't do this again, and we need to see other people. I've spent so much time with you that I haven't gone on dates with anyone else. I want to experience all life has to offer that I've been missing out on."

A cold look settled onto his face, erasing the warmth he'd always looked at her with. "Fine,

Hailey. You have fun experiencing all those things you've missed out on in life."

With that, Cayden left.

Crumbling with sobs that wracked her body, Hailey sank onto a chair, cradling her head in her palms. Just look at what a mess she'd made of her new life, falling for the first man to smile her way.

Fortunately, she'd stepped up to the plate and done what was right for her self-preservation.

Surely, her heart would forgive her when it realized how much pain she'd saved it down the road.

CHAPTER TEN

A MONTH HAD passed and a tired-from-toss-ing-and-turning Hailey arrived at the Venice Has Heart event's medical tent. She'd not seen Cayden yet that morning, but not doing so before the day ended was unavoidable.

Not seeing him made it easier to deceive herself about how tangled up she'd become in the fantasy of being the recipient of his attention.

Her heart had yet to forgive her. So had her body for depriving it of Cayden's magic. She missed him more than she could have imagined. Not that she didn't see him or that he wasn't polite. He was. But he didn't look at her the same. He never met her eyes. Never smiled at her. Never laughed with her. Never texted her funny memes or messages to have "sweet dreams" as she drifted to sleep. Never…never anything because whatever had been between them, they were now only coworkers.

It was what she'd needed to happen, but was still slowly killing her.

Which reinforced that their ending sooner rather than later had been the best thing that could have happened, even if only her logic and self-preservation instinct agreed. Even her friend Jamie had thought Hailey was nuts when she'd revealed that she couldn't be involved with Cayden. Her poor heart wouldn't have survived if she and Cayden had grown any closer. Whether it was going to currently was debatable.

Had anyone ever died from a broken heart? What was she asking? Her own father had died from his broken heart over grieving his wife. Having Hailey in his life hadn't been enough for his will to live to press on. How sad that even for her father she hadn't been enough?

After the change in their relationship, Hailey had briefly considered bailing on the Venice Has Heart event, but she wanted to volunteer and be involved in the community. That had nothing to do with Cayden. She met with the group the previous week, enjoying reconnecting with the Krandalls and Benny, but seeing Cayden smiling and laughing with Leanna had been pure torture. That he'd avoided speaking with Hailey completely had been for the best because she might have burst into tears at how hollow she felt without him in her life.

"Looks as if we've had a great turnout for the run." Having been rushing around helping check runners in and making sure everything was in order, Linda sat down in a folding chair and fanned her tanned face with the torn-off side of a cardboard box. She smiled at Hailey. "Bob and I ran the half marathon this morning before daylight. We didn't want to be slackers."

Hailey didn't think anyone would ever accuse the couple of that.

"How long have you been married?"

"Since I was sixteen and we eloped."

"Sixteen? Was that even legal?" Hailey stared at the women in astonishment. "That's so young."

Linda laughed. "Didn't feel too young and my daddy probably could have forced the issue if he'd wanted. He didn't because he knew I'd been wanting to marry Bob since I was five." Linda's expression brightened with her memories. "He wrote me one of those check yes or no boxes letters asking me to being his girlfriend."

Hailey couldn't help but smile. "I take it you checked the yes box."

Bob stepped up behind his wife and grinned. "That would have been too simple for my Linda. She wrote back asking if I wanted babies and puppies. When I marked yes, she wrote back saying she was going to marry me." He gave his wife an indulgent look. "Who was I to argue with the prettiest girl in class?"

Hailey stared at the couple. "You only dated

each other?" When they nodded, she added, "Didn't you ever wonder if you missed out by not dating anyone else?"

"There was no need to date anyone else when I met the best in kindergarten," Bob assured. "Linda's the only date I wanted. Still is."

Linda patted his cheek. "Ditto, darling."

Hailey watched them with more than a little envy. What would it have been like to have loved and been loved from such a young age? To have grown up knowing that your someone was always there?

They chatted for a few minutes then Bob left to check on where the vendors had set up their booths.

"Isn't he a sweetheart?" Linda asked, watching as he left the tent.

"I'll admit I'm a little jealous."

"He's definitely a keeper." Linda's gaze cut to Hailey. "Is there no one special in your life?"

Face aflame, Hailey fought picking up the cardboard piece Linda had fanned herself with earlier. "I... There was, but we're not involved anymore. It was never going to work. I mean, I miss him, but—" What was she doing? Linda didn't want to hear her pathetic love story. "Yeah, it wouldn't have worked out."

"What makes you think it wouldn't have

worked out? Bad temperament, bad finances, bad breath, or bad sex?"

Hailey's jaw dropped, then managed to say, "None of the above."

"Then, if you miss him as much as it sounds you do, you need to do something to make it work out. Flirt with him a little or something to let him know you're still interested."

"I've never been one of those girls who were natural-born flirters." Not that it would matter if she was. Cayden barely acknowledged she existed these days.

"Just smile and bat those pretty eyes. If it's meant to be, things will work out," Linda advised. "Now, let's double-check our supplies before heading to the main stage for the kickoff. You don't want to miss that."

Yeah, missing Cayden was more than enough.

They were just finishing their check when, clipboard in hand, Cayden walked into the tent.

Hailey's chest tightened. Linda's question echoed through her mind. How had Hailey known it wouldn't work? It just wouldn't have. He was him and she was her. To have continued would have just been delaying the painful inevitable. The only real question had been at what point had she wanted to accept her heartache and refocus on her self-healing and being the best her she could be.

Wearing navy shorts and a Venice Has Heart T-shirt and baseball cap, Cayden was gorgeous. But then, he was no matter what he wore. How could she readily argue his inner beauty was his most stunning attribute when he was so gorgeous on the outside?

What if your best self had been the you who had been with him? her heart whispered before she could hush it.

His gaze went to Linda and didn't budge, almost as if Hailey weren't there. "Anything you ladies need before we officially get started?"

You. For a brief moment, she worried that she'd said her thought out loud. Neither Cayden nor Linda were gawking at her, so she must not have.

"We're good," Linda told him. "No one has needed our services, yet, but that will change once the race gets started. Do you recall last year when those men ran into each other and the one was knocked out cold?"

Hailey was glad Linda continued to chat with Cayden, because it allowed her to try to tamp down her silliness. She did not *need* him. That the thought had entered her head annoyed her. She missed him, a lot, but that didn't mean she needed him.

"Isn't that right?"

Hailey blinked at Linda. Having no idea what she'd just said, she took a cue from her self-help books and smiled. That must have been an okay response. Linda went right back to talking with Cayden until he took off to head back to where Leanna was deejaying the event live on the radio station where she worked.

"Maybe you should try your flirting skills on Dr. Wilton," Linda suggested, causing Hailey to choke on air and have to cough to catch her breath. "He's a great catch."

He was a great catch, but he didn't want to be caught. Hailey coughed again, searching for the right response. Fortunately, Linda laughed and nudged her arm. "Don't look so horrified. It was just a suggestion. Come on. They want us all there for the official kickoff and it's almost time."

Leanna introduced Cayden to the group of volunteers, participants, vendors, and spectators and as with everything, he gave a dynamic motivational pep talk to everyone there. Next, a heart transplant patient who was walking the event said a quick prayer. Cayden wished them all luck and to always have heart.

The official buzzer sounded and the runners were off.

Hailey and Linda made their way back to the medical tent, where Hailey would be most of the day. The first fifteen minutes were slow, but then Cayden arrived on a UTV with one of the runners sitting in the truck bed–type back. Another volunteer drove and, from where he rode beside her, a gloved-up Cayden pressed a bloody gauze pad against the injured woman's knee.

"This is Aimee. She fell and has a pretty nasty gash on her knee from where she hit the pavement," Cayden informed her as he helped the forty-something woman out of the golf cart. As Hailey gloved up, he helped Aimee get settled onto the exam table that had been set up in the tent.

Hailey expected him to leave, but he knelt next to where she had to examine the woman's wound. She pulled off the gauze and winced. "You took a nasty tumble."

"Oh, I'm one of those people who never does anything halfway." Aimee sighed. "I'm not sure what I tripped over. My own feet, I guess, as there was nothing on the pavement."

While Cayden swapped out his gloves, Linda asked questions to fill out a medical encounter form, then had Aimee sign a release.

Apparently planning to assist, he handed a squirt bottle of sterile solution to Hailey. "Saline?"

Did he know it was all she could do to keep her hands from shaking as she took the bottle? Could he hear the thundering of her heart at how near he was?

"Thanks." Taking the bottle, she rinsed the

bleeding wound, clearing out a few stray bits of gravel and wishing she could clean out the wounds of her heart as easily. "The cut is deep and needs sutures to close it."

Aimee winced. "I figured. This isn't my first bout of clumsiness."

"I can send you to the emergency room or I can do the sutures. Your choice," Hailey offered, grateful she'd noted the suture kits in their supplies.

"If you can do it here, then please do." The woman looked relieved that she wasn't going to have to travel elsewhere. "My husband was running ahead of me and doesn't know I fell. He wouldn't complain, but I'd like him to finish the race."

"Gotcha." She glanced toward Cayden. She caught his eyes unexpectedly and her heart ached when her gaze met his and saw a glimmer of something before it disappeared. Her eyes stung with moisture. *Not now*, she scolded herself. Now was not the time to be dwelling on Cayden. Recalling why she'd glanced up, she asked, "Since Aimee told Linda that she's not allergic to anything, could you draw me up a couple of milliliters of lidocaine, please?"

Cayden did so and handed the syringe to her, taking care for their hands not to touch. *No worries, Cayden*, she thought. *Our touching might*

*have rendered me a heaping mess and you'd
have had to sew Aimee's knee without me.*

Changing her gloves over to the ones in the suture kit, Hailey kept her gaze focused on Aimee. She injected the area to anesthetize the skin, activated the needle safety device, then handed the syringe back to him. "I'll close her with the Ethilon number four, please."

Cayden had already pulled out the suture material and dropped it onto the sterile field drape.

Once Aimee was numb, Hailey used the curved needle to put in nine sutures.

"Great job," Cayden praised when she was finished.

Instantly, her eyes prickled with tears again. He was the most positive, uplifting person she'd ever met. Not once had she gotten the impression that he wanted to take over. He was confidently content in her abilities, had been cool with assisting, and had vocalized his appreciation for her skills. He hadn't pointed out that she'd struggled to get that first knot in place because her hands had been shaking. Shaking that hadn't been from lack of belief in herself, but from his nearness. Cayden shook her whole world. He had from the moment she first noticed him from across the hospital cafeteria. If only she'd known then what she knew now, she could have avoided him completely and saved them both a lot of trouble. Only…only, her patient was eyeing her sutured knee.

"Unfortunately, no matter how great of a job, you're going to have a scar, Aimee," she warned the woman, then gave instructions on home care and the need to follow up with her primary care provider for a wound check and suture removal.

When finished, aware of where Cayden was talking with Linda, Hailey disposed of her gloves, then took the medical encounter form that Linda had started to record care provided. Before Hailey finished, the golf cart driver arrived with another runner. Hailey started to stand, thinking she'd finish the simple notation of what she'd done on Aimee's knee later, but Cayden stopped her.

"Linda and I will triage him while you finish your note."

So, willing her hand to be steady, she documented the basics of suturing Aimee's knee, stealing a few glances to where Cayden knelt next to the man sitting on the table Aimee had recently vacated and which Linda had wiped with disinfectant. Kind, gentle, caring, compassionate, all those descriptions and more ran through her mind as she watched Cayden interact with the newcomer, watched him laugh at something the man said when Linda placed a cooling towel on the back of his neck and handed him a sports drink.

Cayden glanced at his watch, then toward her, catching her watching him. His smile faded. He had no smile for her, instead quickly looking back toward the runner, then standing to say something to Linda. Having finished the chart, a wrecked but determined to trudge forward Hailey joined them.

"Roger, here, just needs to cool down. He started out too hard too fast and got overheated. I don't think he's going to need intravenous fluids, but you can keep an eye on him. Leanna messaged that she needs me to join her for the broadcast."

Leanna. Because although Hailey was an emotionally tangled mess, Cayden was used to moving from friends with benefits to just friends or whatever it was they currently were. Maybe eventually they'd be friends like he and Leanna were. Or were he and Leanna in the friends with benefits category? Maybe he'd even eventually prove right all those who believed that when he settled down, it would be with the beautiful deejay.

When he settled down? He had no plans to ever settle down. If he had—she'd what? His willingness to settle down didn't mean he'd have ever chosen Hailey, that he could have ever loved her.

Sighing, she met his gaze and her breath caught that he hadn't moved, but was looking at her with a sad longing that he failed to hide.

Oh, Cayden. Could you have ever grown to love me? Was that even possible, when she'd barely started loving herself and he'd said he no longer believed in love?

Was she truly so gullible, so desperate to be loved, that whatever had been in his eyes made her want to believe in the seemingly impossible?

Cayden had stayed late into the previous night working with his team leaders to make sure they had everything set for the event. With only a few snafus, everything seemed to have gone smoothly. Definitely, the day had been a success, raising needed funds and awareness of heart disease and ways of preventing it within their community. The official activities had ended, and the breakdown and cleanup process had started.

"Cayden?"

Recognizing Hailey's voice, Cayden braced himself. At the hospital he could compartmentalize his interactions with her, could draw upon his professionalism as a shield from the slaying being near her gave him. But, here, he'd lost that edge and had slipped more than once, asking himself over and over what had led to her pushing him away after they'd shared such an intimate connection. What they'd shared had been different, special, addicting. At least, to him. She'd shut him out almost immediately. *Why?*

Had she sensed his growing feelings for her? Sensed that he'd been leading up to telling her that she'd changed his mind—his heart—about so many things and so had pushed him away?

"I know it's been a long day, but are you busy after all this is done?"

Knowing he couldn't just keep standing with his back to her, he sucked in a deep breath and turned to face her. She looked as tired as he felt. He hadn't really anticipated her staying from start to finish, but she'd jumped in to help wherever needed all day. He shouldn't have expected less, not from Hailey.

Maybe she'd been trying to be kind by ending things, afraid she'd hurt him further if they continued. She didn't have to worry. Her reminder of why he didn't get emotionally involved had served its purpose. He'd keep his heart locked away for good this time.

He nodded. "I have plans."

For a moment he thought she was going to turn to leave, but instead, her gaze met his, full of a tumultuous mixture of resignation and forced courage. "With Leanna?"

He nodded. She'd asked him to go eat with her to go over the day's events and to make notes on what worked well and what they could do to improve for next year's event while it was fresh on their minds.

"I… Okay." Why was she looking at him that way? She was the one who'd insisted they end their relationship. "Have a good night then."

Disappointment on her face, Hailey turned to leave. The urge to stop her hit him hard. But he wouldn't. The past month had been difficult. How much harder would it be if he gave in to the urge to beg her to give them another chance? To let him continue with her in the new life she said she was creating for herself?

How crazy was that when she'd let them go so easily? When he'd been about to hand her his heart and she'd shoved the door closed before he could? Three times and he was out. Only, Hailey was nothing like his previous two heartbreaks. Even calling them that felt wrong when they barely registered in comparison to the world-shattering pain Hailey's cutting him out of her life had unleashed. He needed to just let her go.

"Was there something in particular you needed, Hailey?" he asked anyway, causing her to turn back.

She stared at him a moment, then shook her head. "Nothing. Have a good night and thanks again for involving me in today. It was truly a blessing to be here."

She'd been busy in the medical tent with Linda and then with doing heart health consults. She'd taken a few breaks for grabbing something to eat and he'd seen her strolling around to watch the kids playing in the bouncy house, a faraway smile on her face that made him wonder what she was thinking. He'd bet it hadn't been about the things seeing her watching those children had elicited within his bumfuzzled brain. He blamed lack of sleep. Last night and for the whole of the last month. He was physically, mentally, and emotionally exhausted.

"Thank you for volunteering," he found the will to say, even adding, "We hope you'll be back next year."

Her lower lip disappeared into her mouth for a moment, drawing his gaze and eliciting self-disdain at how her tiny gesture twisted him into knots.

"I'll always be there if you need me, Cayden."

Her wording seemed strange and he continued to mull it over while he watched her leave, and he struggled to keep his mind on task during his and Leanna's dinner. She was quick to point that out to him, and when she asked him to her place for drinks, he was quick to say no.

He only wanted one woman and she no longer wanted him in her life.

Grateful for her shower to wash away the day's grime and the tears she'd given in to on her drive home, Hailey towel dried her hair, then put on shorts and a T-shirt to sleep in. It had been a long day, and one with extreme emotions. She'd loved volunteering but being with Cayden outside the hospital setting had highlighted her downward spiral ever since she'd ended their relationship.

Since she'd pushed him away. That was what she'd done. She even knew why. Because he scared her. The way he'd held her, kissed her, touched her, looked into her eyes as he'd made love to her, that had terrified her. Because he made her believe that he cared and she hadn't known how to deal with that. The only two people who had truly cared for her had been gone so long that she'd forgotten how wonderful it felt. It's what she'd craved with John, but never gotten. But Cayden, despite the words he'd said, hadn't held back. He'd nurtured everything good inside her.

Then.

Now he'd cut himself off from her emotionally and was unavailable to her in every way.

Calling herself every kind of fool, she headed to the kitchen, got herself a glass of water, and headed out to her patio. Her gaze immediately went to the lounger. She needed to get rid of the thing because she couldn't look at it and not recall how she'd boldly kissed Cayden, how he'd kissed her back, then made love to her. She'd set her fears aside that night, kissed him and made love to him without any past doubts getting into her head despite there being so many and Cayden had been why. He'd nurtured her confidence, lifted her up to discover the things she hadn't previously learned about herself and life.

She'd moved to Florida to start over from past mistakes and had ended up making the biggest mistake of her life. Because she'd not trusted in what she'd seen happening between them, not trusted in what she saw when he smiled at her, not trusted in her ability to decipher what was real and what she wanted to be real.

Too late she was seeing clearly what she'd had and lost. Question was, what was she going to do about it? Because Florida Hailey refused to go down without a fight. Sure, that she thought she could compete with someone of Leanna's caliber might seem deluded to some, but Cayden hadn't loved Leanna. Not like he had with her. Because she was lovable.

She was. Whether it was months of being away from a man who'd emotionally abused her or doing her therapy and self-healing, she finally realized she was lovable beyond whether or not Cayden ever chose to risk his heart with her again. She was lovable.

Or maybe she was so exhausted that she was delusional. One or the other.

Either way, she had to find Cayden and tell

him everything in her heart. He'd always been easy to talk to, but telling him how she'd let fear hurt them both wouldn't be easy. Could he ever forgive her?

Her doorbell rang. Heart racing, she walked into the house, then peered through the front door's peephole. Cayden! Without thought, she flung the door open and barely prevented herself from flinging herself into her arms.

"You're here." Did he think her strange that she was grinning at him? Why was she grinning? Just because she'd had an epiphany did not mean that he felt any different.

"Can I come in?"

She moved aside, allowing him into her house, watched him automatically start to go out to the patio area, but he changed his mind, stopping in the living area instead.

Mind racing, Hailey followed him there, sitting down on the sofa since he'd taken the chair. "Why are you here, Cayden? I thought you had other plans."

"Leanna had suggested we meet to discuss things we'd do differently or the same at next year's event while it was fresh on our minds. We finished early."

"It wasn't a date?" Happiness filled her. More than it should. Just because his plans with Leanna hadn't been a date didn't mean he was going to forgive and forget that Hailey had been too afraid to let him love her.

"I've not been on a date since with you. I have no interest in dating."

"Oh." Then, sucking in a deep breath and reminding herself that she would be okay no matter what happened, she bared her heart. "Me, either."

His brow lifted. "How are you going to experience all the things you've missed out on in life? The things you couldn't wait to experience?"

Hailey grimaced at the pain she'd caused him. If he'd give her the chance, she'd make it up to him. "I was wrong about what I had missed out on. Dating was never the life experience I was missing out on. Not really."

"No? You'll understand that I find that confusing since that was the reason you gave me for why we couldn't be together."

"Yes, I imagine you do find it confusing." But she was going to lower every wall around her heart and present it to him. Hopefully, since he'd came to her house, that meant all hope wasn't lost. "What I had been missing and never experienced was you, Cayden."

Shock registered on his face, and he swallowed. "Me?"

She nodded. "I gave a decade of my life to a man who was emotionally and mentally abusive. I allowed it to happen. I'd forgive him for doing me wrong, but it never stopped him from doing it again. Probably as a defensive mechanism, I convinced myself that I didn't want to be in a relationship again, that I wanted to be single and free. In reality, it was another relationship like the one I had with John that I didn't want."

"Understandably so." He stared directly into her eyes, making her feel very exposed.

"I know you didn't understand, probably could never understand," she continued, "why I said the things I did on the night we made love." She refused to call it sex ever again. "How could you when you grew up in a loving home where you were always wanted? That wasn't my life. Between foster homes, John, and even with my adopted parents to some degree, I was never necessary." Sweat popped out on her skin and she walked to stand next to where he sat on the sofa. "I convinced myself that in my new life, I was enough, that I didn't need anyone to be complete."

His gaze didn't waver from hers. "You are enough, Hailey. You always were."

"I am," she agreed, kneeling beside him. "From the beginning, I recognized how different you were, Cayden. Just, everything about you. You were so handsome and wonderful that I never gave myself any confidence that you could truly be mine. I didn't think a makeover existed that would allow someone like you to fall for someone like me."

That's when it hit her that she'd washed away all the powders and creams, leaving her face as exposed as her heart. He'd seen her with smudged makeup that she'd replaced the moment she'd felt up to it when he'd taken care of her when she'd been sick. She fought the urge to cover her face with her hands as he studied her face. She needed to do this, to let him see her.

"You're beautiful, Hailey. With or without makeup."

His sincerity warmed her heart because, bless him, he meant what he'd said. She had to reveal everything to him, who she had been along with this new woman she had become and would continue to blossom as.

"You're seeing the makeup-less version that still has lash and hair extensions and fillers. I'll be right back." She went to her bedroom, got a box down from the top of her closet. She carried it into the living room and set it down on the coffee table. Her hands trembled as she lifted the lid to reveal the contents of her former life. The last photo she'd taken with her adoptive parents was on top and her heart ached with missing them. They had loved her and for that she'd forever be grateful. They'd given her a home and family, even if it hadn't lasted nearly long enough. She picked up the photo and handed it to Cayden. "This is me. The real me who didn't believe you could ever love her and so she convinced herself she didn't want love or forever. The me who was so scared of what was happening between us that I destroyed the most precious gift I've ever known."

Still reeling that he'd driven to Hailey's rather than going home, reeling at the things Hailey was saying when he'd wondered if she'd even let him into her house, Cayden took the photo, stared at the pretty young woman staring back at him, and wondered what all the fuss was about. Sure, Hailey's hair and lashes were different. Her lips weren't as full, and her beautiful eyes were hidden behind a thick pair of glasses. Reaching into the box, he pulled out other photos, mostly school pictures which were never the most flattering, but even with those, her beauty came through. He glanced through the stack, coming across only one that was of her and a man who must be her ex.

He tapped the photo. "How old are you here?"

Her gaze was glued to the photo. "Eighteen. I thought I was the luckiest girl alive that John was interested in me. I got rid of the other photos of us. There weren't many considering how long we were together. I kept this one as a reminder that once upon a time, I thought he loved me and that I'd never be alone again. Clinging to that is what led to me staying in a bad relationship. I kept the picture to remind myself to never let anyone close enough to me for them to hurt me ever again."

He fought the urge to crumple the photo, but tossed it back into the box. "Maybe I should have kept pictures."

"It didn't work, anyway."

Knowing she meant him, Cayden flinched. "Hurting you in any way was never my intention."

She shook her head. "You didn't hurt me, Cayden. My holding on to the past that I came here to put behind me is what hurt me." She gave an ironic laugh and swiped at her watery eyes. "I changed my outer appearance because I wanted to be different. Sure, I was doing the therapy sessions, but I was still prisoner to the inner me who didn't feel lovable and so if I convinced myself I didn't want to be loved, then I could pretend my shiny new outer appearance was lovable."

He gestured to the photo. "You were never unlovable, Hailey. The woman in those photos is you and, of her, your lovability, I have no doubts."

Her smile was offset by her tears. "Thank you. You're the kindest person I know."

He snorted. "You think I'm being kind?" He shook his head and stood, bringing her up from where she'd knelt with him. He lifted her chin so he could look directly into her eyes. "Saying that you are lovable isn't me being kind. It's me telling you the truth."

More tears slid down her cheek and this time when she went to wipe them away, he caught her hand with his and laced their fingers. Bending, he kissed her wet cheek. "Don't cry, Hailey. I never want you to cry."

"I'm sorry, Cayden. About everything. I've messed everything up, haven't I?"

He shook his head. "The fake lashes and hair will eventually all fall out and you'll be back to yourself."

Confused, she stared at him. "That's not what I meant."

"Nor maybe what I should have said. I want you happy. I want you to look in the mirror and see the most beautiful, wonderful woman in the world. If those things help you to see what I see, then by all means, keep them. Do them for *you*, because they make you happy, but not because of your perception of anyone else's standards."

"I—okay. Now you sound like my therapist."

"What does your therapist say?"

"That I should use whatever tools necessary to rebuild my inner power and once I've rebuilt it, then I get to choose which tools I keep and which I toss aside."

"Smart therapist." He studied her, taking in every feature, every nuance of her face. "You embracing your inner power is going to a beautiful thing to behold, Hailey."

"I—when that happens, will you be a part of my life, Cayden? Not just at work, but in all of my life? I was wrong to push you away when all I really wanted was to hold you so tightly that you'd never leave. I've regretted doing so every moment since, no matter how much I tried to convince myself I'd done the right thing."

Hope had been building in Cayden from the moment she'd opened the front door and smiled at him. Hope that demolished the makeshift walls he'd put around his heart. He could never defend his heart from her, not when she owned it.

"Haven't you figured it out yet, Hailey? I know how lovable you are because I love you. Completely, thoroughly, and to utter distraction. It's not anything about your outer appearance, but about what's in here." He lifted their laced hands to where he could press his finger to her heart, then grazed his knuckles across her temple. "And about what's in here. So much so that no matter how much I tried to keep my heart locked away, reminding myself of past betrayals, I fell for you anyway because you are unlike any person I have ever known. My heart knew that long before I acknowledged how I felt." He took a deep breath and looked straight into her eyes. "I love you, Hailey."

Hailey could barely believe what she was hearing. Was it even possible that he loved her?

"I didn't know." Staring at him in awe, she started over. "Maybe, I did know, Cayden. Because I felt safe with you, enough so that I told you things I'd never told anyone. Enough so that I showed you those photos and deep down, I knew it was okay to show you, that you wouldn't be repulsed."

"The only photo that did was the one with you next to the wrong man."

Happiness filling her, more than she'd once dreamed possible, she asked, "Are you the right man?"

"For you? You better believe it."

Wrapping her arms around him, Hailey hugged him, so grateful for the strong beat of his heart against her cheek. "I do."

"I should warn you that someday I'm going to want to hear you say those words to me again. We'll wait until you're ready, until you see forever in the way you've made me view it, but with you, Hailey, a lifetime will never be enough."

Hailey's heart might explode with joy from what she saw in his eyes. Love. Forever. That fidelity he'd mentioned. It was all there and more. She knew because all those things had to be shining back at him as he looked into her eyes. "Someday, I'd like to say those words to you again. You and you alone."

Then Cayden was kissing her, and all Hailey could think was that this must be what happy-ever-after felt like, because she was positive that was exactly what it was.

* * * * *

If you enjoyed this story, check out these other great reads from Janice Lynn

Risking it All with the Paramedic
Breaking the Nurse's No-Dating Rule
Heart Doctor's Summer Reunion
The Single Mom He Can't Resist

All available now!